AF405938

Book 3 in The Woodcarver's Quilt series

A Christmas Rose

A Novella by
J. Linde

A Christmas Rose is dedicated to:

All medical personnel who see and support those
involved in Domestic violence.
The Hotlines that help and keep confidential any
caller seeking help.
John for being one of my kids and helping cut
out, route, laminate, and provide valuable
information in building the rocking horse.
My daughter, Rebecca, for the hours of
designing and creating the cover page, and
even more, hours editing the novella; for
guiding and often nudging me to think deeper
to bring the story alive.
And most of all, to you, my readers.

Have a Blessed and Safe Christmas Season!

-J. Linde

Table of Contents

Chapter 1

A Voice from Yesteryear

Tobiah walked through the enormous sliding doors leading to the inner sanctum of Yoder's Mill, located on the outer edges of the old Yoder farmstead. He greeted each of his men; it was something he did every morning, taking a personal interest in each of his employees. The mill Foreman received a more focused part of this one-on-one as they discussed the strategies for the day. Then, and only then, Tobiah made his way to his office centrally located within the Mill.

From his office, Tobiah only had to glance out of one of the many windows to have a bird's eye view of the whole work floor. The head rig took up the entire northwest section of the building; a gas generator kept its massive eight-foot blade moving with purpose. Logs, greater than the circumference of a horse, were easily ripped in two as they were fed into the blade's sharp teeth. Looking to the east, Tobiah noted some men were stacking rough-cut lumber in preparation to make deliveries. Off to the south, he realized there were still freshly timbered trees needing to be fed through the blade.

'Tamorrow, another shipment of logs will be here. An area outside the slidin' doors needs ta be cleared ta store them.' Tobiah nodded with satisfaction, and although he expected the men to have the area cleared by the end of the day, he insisted on safety first. He understood if it meant some of the men had to stay late to get the area cleared. He would work with them to ensure that the job was done right. It was no time to cut corners, which invariably led to accidents.

Yoder's Mill was well known for its quality lumber and the craftsmanship of the men that worked there. His crews raised barns, repaired storm-damaged buildings, and restored older homes. They worked on everything, from the foundation to the roof – and everything in between. Tobiah had little need to advertise; word of mouth and the work ethics of the Amish were all the advertising needed. Most often, Tobiah Yoder and his work crews were hard-pressed to keep up with the demand.

Tobiah glanced over at his desk. The continuous blinking on the answering machine meant there were messages, causing him to smile. More work assured his men of jobs, and more jobs resulted in a healthy and thriving Amish community. He rolled out the solid oak office chair, took a seat, and pulled a pad of paper and pencil toward him. Punching the playback button, he began listening to the messages.

The first message confirmed the delivery of logs from northern Ontario. Their estimated delivery time was between ten and twelve the following day. Without fail, the logging company always called the day before they made the delivery. Tobiah made a mental note to remind his foreman of the delivery. There were two messages requesting estimates. With a carpenter's sense of accuracy and detail, he wrote down each caller's contact number, address, and name. Knowing how busy his men would be with the incoming delivery, he'd need to ask Jed Kuepfer to go with him and take measurements for those estimates.

Tobiah sat back in his chair with a feeling of satisfaction; he couldn't be happier with the mill's success. Reaching forward, he pressed the button again to listen to the one remaining message.

His heart stopped for the space of a second before it started racing as the message played. Blood drained from his usually ruddy complexion, and his palms became sweaty.

It was a voice he hadn't heard in more than three years, nor had he expected to ever again. The last time he had listened to that voice, the conversation had ended in querulous, demanding words – on his part. Repeatedly, over the years, he had regretted not bridling his tongue. Ultimately, it resulted in animosity between himself and his wife, Miriam. It had taken months for them to get back on track as a married couple. Unexpected tears rushed to his eyes, and he knew he would do anything to put wrongs right. How many times had he prayed to God to give him another chance? Now, in all His great mercy, God had heard and answered his prayers. He listened intently to the message. The ending was abrupt, like something had happened to cut it short. There was no phone number, but he had enough on which to act.

"*Dat*, it's me. I got hurt, and I was hoping you could help us. Can you *kumme* before three?"

Tobiah scribbled down the address, unwilling to rely on his memory and afraid the message would get erased before he could get it written down. The announcement was chopped off, "You'll like Seth; he's such a neat…."

Suddenly, and annoyingly the answering machine became silent.

Tobiah played and replayed the message, hoping her words would go on each time. "My Rosie, my little Rosie." Tears flowed unchecked down his face, and he glanced at the clock on the office wall - Nine-thirty. Quickly, he dialed the number of the man who usually drove them long distances and was relieved when Bob picked up on the third ring. On the other end, the man informed him. "I can't go today, Tobiah, but I should be able to fit it in tomorrow. I have a trip tomorrow morning early, but I'll try to be there around noon to drive you to Mississauga."

There was a prolonged silence on Tobiah's end as his brain wheeled over his options. "I need ta go taday. I'll get back ta ya, later." He slammed down the receiver without saying goodbye, immediately going over the situation in his mind. 'Should I tell Miriam that Rosie called? I can't. She went ta Ruthie's this mornin'.' He rapped his knuckles on the desk. 'Maybe the man that drives Jed can take me.' Dialing the number to the phone in Jed's phone shanty, he waited impatiently - not surprised, there was no answer. Hurrying out of his office, he raced down the steps and ran to Jed's farm on the other side of the road. The entire way there, his thoughts remained on overdrive. 'Who is Seth? Did Rosie get married? How did she get to Mississauga?'

Images of his middle child, Rosie, flitted through his thoughts. Rosie, with her ready smile. And the times Rosie ran to meet him when he came home from work each afternoon. Finally, Rosie, an eighteen-year-old, tears streaming down her face the day he had forbidden her to go to an amusement park. Tobiah knew he had driven her away;

that had been the last he and Miriam had ever seen her. She'd be twenty-one now, soon to be twenty-two. She'd be coming back all grown up, provided she returned. Mentally, he relived the telephone message, each word etched in his thoughts and on his heart.

Jed saw his long-time friend coming quickly up the lane. He chuckled to himself. Tobiah was always on the move. His smile faded when he realized he'd never seen Tobiah run anywhere. The closer Tobiah got, the more Jed realized something wasn't quite right. He frowned as Tobiah made a sudden turn toward the phone shanty.

Out of breath, Tobiah called out as he hurried past his friend. "I need the number ta yer long-distance driver!"

"The number's inside; his name's George." Jed answered and hung back, giving Tobiah privacy to make his call.

Afterward, Jed stood in the yard with his old friend, making small talk. Tobiah was so preoccupied with his thoughts that he didn't notice how Jed studied him. Jed could see that all was not well with Tobiah, but he knew that eventually, his friend would let him in. "*Kumme* give me a hand with the buggy. Eva needs ta go inta town with Esther." They stood under the old maple waiting for the women to come out.

Esther and Eva walked past them and greeted Tobiah before climbing into the buggy. They were carrying more quilts to the Amish store in town. Tobiah glanced at Esther, reminded that she was the same age as Ruthie, younger by one year than Rosie. Why, oh why, hadn't he let Rosie go with her friends? Esther had gone on *rumspringa* and had returned, so why hadn't he given Rosie the benefit of the doubt? Tobiah passed a hand over his eyes. Jed was saying something, and he looked blankly at his old friend, trying to recall what he had said.

"Somethin' not sittin' right with ya, Tobiah?"

Tobiah nodded and confided in his long-time friend. Somehow, getting this burden off his chest made him feel better.

"So, George'll be here at one taday?" Jed asked.

Tobiah nodded in affirmation.

Jed nodded, unsure of what to say. "How'd be we wait 'til next week ta measure them jobs ya mentioned? It'll give ya the rest of this week ta see ta family matters. Ya want me ta do chores fer ya later taday?"

"*Ja.* In case I'm not back in time. Could ya check in with Miriam when ya do them? But let me tell her about Rosie."

"*Ja.* I'll keep an eye on things. I'll let you do the explainin' ta Miriam. Could be yer *kummin'* back with yer Rosie?" Jed smiled optimistically at Tobiah.

"*Ja.* Could be." A cautious smile tugged at the corners of Tobiah's mouth. "That'd be *gut*. Ain't?" He sighed.

"I'd say." Jed smiled. "I couldn't imagine bein' without Esther," he thought aloud, sad at the prospect of not having his daughter. 'Adoptin' Esther an' Eli was the best thing that ever happened ta Eva an' me – ta *Mamm* an' *Daed* too.'

As if knowing Jed's thoughts, Tobiah nodded. "But ya near didn't get them."

"*Ja*, but I listened ta my *gut* friend's advice, an' I've never regretted it. *Danke*."

Tobiah nodded absently and began walking down the lane, thinking, 'I need ta tell my foreman I'll be away.' Then as if comprehending Jed's words, he called over his shoulder. "Yer *willkommen*."

"I'll walk out with ya ta see what's fer mail," Jed hurried after him. The two old friends walked out the drive together, noticeably slower than when Tobiah had come in.

~ ~ ~

Blessed are the merciful, for they shall obtain mercy.
~ Matthew 5:7 ~

CHAPTER 2
Angels Watch Over Thee

Jed's driver, George, arrived later than expected. After one o'clock, he pulled his van up to the Mill. Tobiah was so relieved to finally see the van that he stopped his agitated pacing and raced toward it, yanking the door open before the vehicle could stop. Climbing into the front passenger seat, he buckled the seat belt and handed the piece of paper he'd scribbled Rosie's address on to George.

The man looked at the address. "This is further away than I thought, Tobiah. Are you sure you don't want to leave the trip for another time?"

"*Nee*. I need ta go taday, an' I need ta be there by three." Tobiah knew he'd never make it through the night if he had to wait until the next day to get to Rosie.

George looked at Tobiah questioningly. He'd driven this man from time to time, and each time Tobiah had been cheerful and upbeat. But not so today, so he assured as kindly as he could. "If traffic is good, we might, but we'll get there one way or another." He pulled out onto the dirt road, which led them to a hard-topped highway, finally merging onto the multi-lane 401 highway that would ultimately take them toward Mississauga, just west of Toronto.

Tobiah kept looking at the clock on the dashboard of the van. He had a sinking feeling they wouldn't get to the address; Rosie had left in her message before three. But how could George be faulted? The man was driving as fast as he could.

"Do you have an appointment at this address, Tobiah?" George finally broke the tense silence that loomed between the two men.

"*Ja*. My *tochter* Rosie lives there, an' she got hurt an' needs my help."

George nodded. "I'll do my best to get you there." At three-forty, he pulled the van up to a long row of run-down townhouses, which had been used to house military families years before. They were tired old buildings that someone had bought up, squeezing one last bit of money out of them. The city was on the verge of bulldozing them down, and rightfully so; they were nothing more than impending death traps.

"Are you sure this is the right address?" George looked at the piece of paper Tobiah had handed him earlier. "It doesn't look like a very good neighborhood."

"*Ja*. I'm sure. I listened ta the message more than once."

"Well, then this is it," George peered skeptically out the window at the house number dangling beside an open door. A man sat on a wooden chair, naked from the waist up, a beer bottle in one hand and a cigarette in the other. The muscles on his arms and chest bulged with each swig of the bottle, making one realize it wouldn't be prudent to get on his wrong side. "Why don't you ask that fella? He seems like he knows his way around. I'll stay here and keep the van running," George suggested. Tobiah looked at him sideways, knowing precisely why George didn't want to leave the van's safety.

He opened the door, climbed out, and approached the large man. "I'm lookin' fer Rose."

"What do ya want her for, old man?" The man sat upright in the chair, causing the front legs to hit the wood floor of the porch with a smack as he stopped balancing it on its back legs.

"I'm her *daed, kumme* ta say *hallo*."

"Yeah. I can see that. Ya have that same dumb way of talkin' that she has." He turned and hollered through the open door. "Hey, Rose! There's some old codger out here ta see ya. Says he's yer old man." He took a swig of beer. "Rose!" He bellowed louder.

"*Ja*. I'm here, Dennis," came a timid voice from inside the house's darkness.

Dennis jabbed a thumb toward Tobiah.

"Hi *Dat*," Rosie whispered, visibly on the verge of crying.

"Rosie. *Ach* Rosie." Tobiah, devastated, shook his head at how his daughter looked; she was nothing more than a bag of bones and covered with bruises everywhere he could see.

Rosie looked nervously at Dennis. "Dennis, I called my *daed* to come and get Seth. I'm havin' a hard time lookin' after him with my broken arm, an' all."

Dennis looked from Rosie to Tobiah, and his eyes gleamed in contemplation. "Ya can have the brat fer all I care. All it does is snivel and whine anyway. But you ain't goin' nowheres," he sneered, jabbing his finger in Rosie's face.

"I'll stay here with you, Dennis. I just find it hard lookin' after Seth right now. That's all," her voice petered off.

"I never wanted him anyway," he slurred and guzzled back the rest of the beer. He threw the empty bottle onto the lawn – or what was left of a yard, careful to avoid the large motorcycle parked there.

"*Dat,* just wait here, and I'll get Seth." Rosie turned wild eyes toward Dennis and hurried into the house.

Minutes later, Rosie returned, leading a little boy by the hand. "*Dat,* this is Seth."

Dennis slammed a foot on one of the wooden planks beneath his feet and hollered at the child. Everyone jumped, startled by such belligerent behavior. Dennis guffawed, amused by his cruel prank. The little boy began crying and attempted to sidle away from the great bully.

Rosie positioned herself between Dennis and her child. She talked soothingly to Seth, encouraging him as she led him past Dennis. As they neared the van, she reverted to her mother tongue, their dialect of German. "Please, *Dat,* take him and keep him for me."

"I can't leave ya here, Rosie girl," Tobiah protested.

"Just go," she pleaded. "Before he changes his mind."

"I'm *kummin'* back fer ya."

"*Ja, Dat,* but before three. Ya have ta *kumme* before three." Rosie backed away from the van and waved to her little boy.

"What's all that mumbo jumbo about?" Dennis demanded. "Get back inta the house before I break yer other arm," he growled and stood threateningly over her until Rosie scurried away to do his bidding.

Tobiah sat in the seat behind George, holding the crying baby, while Seth repeatedly called, "Mama. Mama."

"We need to go," George's voice held an element of fear.

"*Ja*. Go before he gets more upset," Tobiah urged. He turned to look out the back window and saw Dennis sit back down on the chair, another beer in hand, but he couldn't see Rosie anywhere. Turning his attention to the crying child. "It's goin' ta be okay. Tamorrow, we'll go get yer Mama." To George, he added. "I need ya ta bring me back tamorrow."

George's worried eyes met Tobiah's in the rearview mirror. "Are you sure, Tobiah?"

"*Ja*. I need ta get my *tochter* outa there. As long as we *kumme* before three, we'll be okay. He'll be at work."

George gave a great sigh of trepidation. "Alright," he finally agreed, but under his breath, he promised himself, 'But if he's there, I won't be stopping."

Seth finally fell asleep in Tobiah's arms, cheeks still wet from his tears, emitting the occasional hiccup. It was close to seven in the evening when George dropped them off. "I'll be here at noon tomorrow," he informed Tobiah as Tobiah paid him for the day's trip.

"I'll be waitin'," Tobiah promised and closed the door with one hand while holding Seth securely in his other arm.

Miriam came rushing out of the house. "Tobiah, I've been so worried about you." She stopped, a frown pulling her brows together. She looked at Seth, noting the familiar reddish-blonde hair, then back at Tobiah. "Who's that?"

"This is Seth. He's our *enkel.*"

"Our grandchild?" Miriam asked, baffled. She felt like she was looking at a younger version of her husband, but where Tobiah's face was round – a result of Miriam's good cooking, Seth's was thin and sallow, his eyes sunken from malnutrition and distress.

"*Ja*. Rosie's *boppli.*"

Miriam felt her world stop before looking behind Tobiah. "Rosie?"

"She's not here, but she will be tamorrow. I'm goin' back ta get her."

Seth began to whimper - slowly waking up, calling, "Mama."

Miriam's maternal instincts came to the fore, and she took the child from Tobiah's arms, cooing to soothe his tears. "*Kumme* and have something to eat. I was worried sick about you." She led the way into the house.

Miriam and Tobiah spent a sleepless night; Seth was a restless sleeper and frequently woke to call for Rosie. At daybreak, Miriam, worried sick about Rosie, unloaded a barrage of questions onto Tobiah. "I wish you could have brought Rosie with you."

"*Ja*. But taday I'm goin' ta be bringin' her home no matter what."

"How does she look?"

"Thin. She needs some of yer *gut* cookin'."

"How did you know where to go?"

"She left a message on the phone at the Mill office."

"Why didn't you tell me?"

"Ya had gone ta Ruthie's when I got the message."

"I'll *kumme* with you when you go get Rosie."

"*Nee*, it's best ya stay here an' look after Seth."

Miriam looked at him disheartened, but she knew Tobiah was right. At that point, she didn't think she could trust anyone with her grandson – he was one step closer to her Rosie coming home. Finally, she nodded, conceding.

Tobiah pushed away from the breakfast table. "If'n ya can manage Seth, a load of logs will be delivered taday, an' I need ta make sure the Mill has a place ta store them before I leave."

"*Ja*. Seth and I will get along fine. But we'll be a lot better when Rosie gets here."

Tobiah nodded and muttered, "We all will." Instead of taking his usual route to the Mill, he deviated and ended up at the Kuepfer farm.

Finding Jed watering the horses, Tobiah shared the previous day's events. "I was wonderin' if'n ya could find the time to go with me? Rosie's in a really bad way."

"*Ja*. I'll go with ya. Let me tell Eva I'll be meetin' ya at the Mill around noon."

A few minutes past noon, George pulled up to the Mill and, within seconds, was back on the road, Tobiah and Jed still buckling up. They were making good time when suddenly, the traffic came to a grinding halt; it proceeded in stop-and-go fashion for the next half hour.

"We need to find another route," George drummed his fingers on the steering wheel. "Or it'll take us a month of Sundays to get there."

Tobiah and Jed watched as he reached over and extracted a much-used map from the glove box. "There's a smaller highway that branches off from the 401. If I can find where they intersect, it might be worth giving it a try."

He reached over again and pulled a newer map out of the glove box. "Here it is," he traced the route with his index finger. "It'll be close," George studied the directions on the newer map. "The best route is to take the 403 to the Gardner Expressway."

'Cutting it close' was the understatement of the year. George pulled his van up to the front of the rundown building at two fifty-five. Tobiah jumped out of the van and pounded on the door. Jed followed, looking questioningly at the dismal buildings. He quickly surveyed them with a critical eye. Nothing, in his estimation, could be done with them to make them functional again.

A woman living in the attached townhouse opened her door a crack. "What do you want?" She demanded.

"I've *kumme* ta get my *tochter*," Tobiah informed her and pounded on the weather-worn door again.

"Huh? Your what?"

"His daughter," Jed translated.

The woman opened her door a little wider. "Yeah? Rosie?"

"*Ja*, Rosie," Tobiah confirmed, still banging on the door.

Flinging her door open, she urged. "The steel factory is about to change shifts, and he'll be home soon. You better hurry! You have ten minutes, at the most, to get her out of here." No sooner had the words left her mouth than the men heard a long shrill whistle. The woman ran over to bang on the door. "Rosie, hurry," she called out. "Your dad's here to get you." When there was no answer, the woman looked at Tobiah frantically. "If you want to take her with you, you'll have to break down this door." Tobiah looked at her as if she had lost her mind.

Frustrated, she pressed, "He beat her something terrible after you left yesterday. Maybe she's even dead!"

At that, Tobiah put his shoulder to the rickety old door and gave a shove. It swung open with little persuasion. The woman ran into the room and knelt beside an inert form on the floor.

"Rosie. Rosie," she pleaded, gently shaking the unresponsive body, then began crying at the sight of a pool of blood on the floor. "Hurry, you have to get her out of here." She snatched a dirty sheet from the couch and began wrapping her in it. "Oh, dear God," she gasped and picked up a tiny limp form beside Rosie. "He killed her baby!" She cried. "He's nothin' but a murderer!" Quickly she bundled the lifeless form into the sheet along with Rosie.

Tobiah stood white-faced, staring at his daughter's limp figure. He knelt beside Rosie; tears streamed down his face - clouding his vision. He tried to gather her to him, but her body was overly pliant in her unconscious state, making it impossible for Tobiah to lift her from the floor. If Jed hadn't come to the rescue, it's unlikely Tobiah could have raised her alone. Once she was in his arms, Tobiah hugged her close and ran out of the house.

The neighbor ran ahead and opened the van door.

"Did you call the police?" George demanded, seeing all the blood.

"Are you crazy? The police never come to this neck of the woods," she shot back at him. "Hurry!" She spurred, wild-eyed, "I hear his bike coming." She slammed the door shut behind Tobiah. Throwing advice over her shoulder as she ran back to her house, "Go the other way, or you'll run into him going that way." She bolted the door to her apartment as George made an abrupt U-turn in the narrow street. He tore down the road, taking a side alley just as Dennis came up the street on his chopper. The curtains on the woman's window closed as she made a hasty retreat to the other end of her house and quickly washed the blood from her hands at the kitchen sink. That was the last thing she needed, tell-tale signs that she had helped Rosie and her dad escape.

George had no idea where he was going. After ten minutes of driving, he found a McDonald's where he could study his map and ask strangers for directions. Within minutes he was pointed in the right direction and on the road again. Heaving a deep sigh, it was evident he was badly shaken, but no more so than Tobiah and Jed. "Do you want to take her to the hospital?" He glanced over his shoulder at Tobiah.

"I'm afraid ta. That's one of the first places he'll look fer her. Can ya take me home, an' I'll get ya ta stand by fer a bit 'til my *frau* an' me decide what we should do?"

"You betcha," George nodded and concentrated on getting his passengers home as fast as possible.

Two hours later, George pulled up to the Yoder homestead; Miriam came barging out of the kitchen door. A strangled cry escaped her throat when she saw the blood all over Tobiah and Jed and the sheet-soaked crimson.

Tobiah explained Rosie's situation and the day's events as quickly as he could. Miriam, generally not a hysterical woman collected her wits and took control, giving instructions to Tobiah and Jed. "*Kumme,* Tobiah, bring her into the *haus*. Jed, I need you to go and get Anna Woerner; she'll know what to do," she assured him.

After laying Rosie on a bed upstairs, Tobiah went down the steps; grateful George had taken Jed to the Woerner's. He hastened to gather the items Miriam asked him to collect. First, he stoked the fire in the wood stove and then boiled a pot of water. Quickly, he flew back up the stairs and grabbed the clean sheets Miriam had requested. He called out softly, knocking on the door before opening it a crack.

Miriam met him at the door.

"How is she?" He inquired, handing the sheets to his wife.

Miriam's stricken expression said everything, "I hope Anna gets here soon."

Within minutes Jed was knocking on the door of the *Dawdi haus* belonging to Charles and Anna Woerner.

When Anna saw all the blood on Jed's shirt, she threw the door wide. "Are you hurt?" She searched his face.

"*Nee*. It's Rosie, Tobiah's girl. She's in a bad way. Can ya *kumme*?"

Anna snatched up her bag with medical supplies, usually used when she helped women giving birth. She called her husband, Charles, and added more medical supplies to her bag. "I'm on my way to the Yoder's on an emergency. It may be morning before I get back."

Charles stepped into the kitchen and saw the blood all over Jed's shirt. Concerned, he asked, "Ya hurt, Jed?"

"*Nee*. It's Tobiah's girl, Rosie." His face contorted. "She's in a bad way."

"Ya best go," Charles directed to Anna. "If'n ya don't get back *tanacht*, I'll *kumme* fer ya in the mornin'."

While George drove back to the Yoder's, Jed quickly told Anna about Rosie and what he thought had happened to her. "I expect Tobiah an' Miriam will want ya ta give her a *gut* check over. If'n ya think she should go ta the hospital, I'll get George ta stand by an' take her."

"*Ja*. I'll check her over. Sometimes losing a *boppli* before it's ready to be born can make things look worse than they are."

An hour later. Anna made her way wearily down the steps. "I was able to get the bleeding stopped." She informed Tobiah. "She's weak and has a broken arm."

"*Ja*. When I went to get Seth, she had that yesterday, " Tobiah informed her.

Anna nodded and went on. "Whoever beat her didn't plan on her living. Besides being severely malnourished, I'd say you did a *gut* thing, getting her and the boy out of there. Her newborn came too early, and she didn't make it."

"*Danke*, Anna. Tell me what I owe ya, an' I'll get it to ya."

"That's not to worry about just now," Anna assured him.

"Ya don't suppose she should go ta the hospital, do ya?" Tobiah looked worriedly at her.

"*Nee*. She'll recover better with Miriam looking after her."

"*Danke*," Tobiah nodded, deep in thought. "Can I get Jed's driver ta take ya back home?"

"*Ja*, if you would. I'll *kumme* and check on Rosie tomorrow. I expect you'll be in touch with Bishop about the little one."

"*Ja*. I wonder if she was born alive?" Tobiah frowned.

"Rosie came around for a few minutes and said the *boppli* made little whimpering sounds but was quiet soon after. A *boppli* can't live very long when they're only seven months along. They aren't developed well enough to survive without oxygen and being kept warm in an incubator."

Tobiah nodded and passed a hand over his eyes. "*Danke*, Anna. *Kumme* an' I'll get Jed an' George ta drive ya home." He paid the driver and looked at Jed. "I'll talk ta ya tamorrow. *Danke* fer *kummin'*. I don't know what I woulda done without yer help."

Jed nodded. "If'n ya need us *tanacht*, we're only across the road."

Tobiah nodded, watched the van go out the drive, then turned wearily and slowly climbed the steps. He stood in the doorway of Rosie's old room. Miriam sat quietly in the rocking chair; glancing up, she saw Tobiah standing there and went to him.

"Will you get in touch with Bishop tomorrow, so we can make arrangements to bury Rosie's *boppli*?" Miriam began to weep.

"*Ja*." Tobiah took her in his arms. "First thing in the mornin'. Are ya stayin' here beside our girl?"

"*Ja*. Just in case she needs something."

Tobiah nodded his head, so overwhelmed he couldn't speak.

"You did a *gut* thing getting her and Seth out of that situation. *Danke,* Tobiah."

Tobiah nodded. "I'll bring ya somethin' ta eat an' an extra blanket."

They held each other for a few minutes more, then hastened to their different posts.

~.~.~.~

Three days later, on a dismal wet day, a tiny casket was lowered into the hard, dark ground. Rosie sat in a chair surrounded by her family and wept. When it was time to leave, Tobiah picked his daughter up and settled her in the family buggy. It was hard for them to leave behind one of their own, especially when there was no need for it to have happened.

In the days following, Tobiah had difficulty living with himself; he placed the blame squarely on his own shoulders. If he hadn't driven his daughter away those many months ago, none of them would be enduring this grief.

~ ~ ~

...despise not one of these little ones;
For I say unto you, in heaven their
angels always behold the face of my Father
~ Matthew 18:10 ~

Chapter 3

In Paths of Righteousness

It was a long and rocky road to recovery for Rosie. Her body was malnourished, and her physical and emotional state had run the gauntlet as well. Some things would never leave her - insisting on plaguing her for years to come. Where once she had been a self-confident young woman, a trait encouraged from the time she was tiny by her parents, Rosie now second-guessed herself. She was full of self-doubt and continually looked to others for approval in accomplishing the smallest of tasks. On *rumspringa,* wearing tight jeans and skimpy tops made her feel appealing. She would flip her waist-length blonde hair saucily over her shoulder and walk with a jaunty air of recklessness. Engulfed in her rebellious attitude, Rosie accomplished what she'd set out to do – gain independence. Unfortunately, that defiant streak attracted the wrong kind of companions, case in point – Dennis. It was too late before she realized her folly and often wished she could return home to the quiet, unassuming ways of the Amish. At first, obstinance prevented her from going home, but then circumstances began dictating a way of life she came to hate. Finally, she swallowed her pride and called for help – not for herself, but because she was frightened for her little boy's well-being. She convinced herself she would survive, but Seth deserved to be raised by a stable family, and the only stability she knew was what her parents had provided for herself and her sisters.

Now, she was home - where she and Seth could begin their journey to emotional and physical well-being. Nights were often riddled with terrifying dreams, leading to days tormented with the possibility of those dreams coming true. So much so that she kept Seth to herself for the longest time, closeted in the house, afraid that Dennis would find them one day.

Seth clung to Rosie. She was the one consistent person in his short life. In turn, Rosie clung to him, even insisting Seth sleep in the bedroom with her. She kept him close, afraid of losing him like she had lost her baby girl. In the process, Rosie smothered her son by over-protecting him. Regardless of her attempts to protect them, they were startled by sudden, abrupt sounds. At night, the loud thunderstorms booming had Rosie waking in cold sweats and Seth screaming. Miriam would rush to Rosie's bedside to calm her while Tobiah lifted the frightened tot from his crib. He walked the floor, soothing the toddler with comforting words and rubbing his back consolingly.

Anna and Miriam continued to devote many hours to rebuilding Rosie's health. During this time, they encouraged her to get outside. The days spent in the sunshine and wandering beside the Mill pond helped Rosie lose her gauntness. Her arm began to heal, and daily household chores strengthened the wasted muscles. With Miriam's nourishing food, Rosie and Seth soon became stronger in body and spirit.

Often Esther walked across the road to visit, sometimes bringing Eva and May. Rosie was always fond of May, thinking of her as the grandmother she never had. May smiled kindly at the little girl she had watched grow into womanhood. Where once Rosie's hair shone like sunshine on a wheat field, it now hung limp and dull. Bright, energetic eyes now held an element of fear, but if May noticed these things, she uttered not a word. Instead, she held Rosie in her arms with a warm embrace and rubbed her back. "It's so *gut* to see you."

Rose just nodded, tears rolling down her face at May's welcomed show of affection. May held her at arms-length, smiling lovingly at her. Attempting to gain control of her emotions, Rosie blurted the first thing that came into her head. "I always enjoyed making cookies with you and Esther."

"*Ja*. We had *gut* times baking cookies for your *daed*. Do you remember measuring a cup of salt instead of sugar?" May's eyes sparkled with amusement.

"*Ach*. I hoped you would have forgotten about that," Rosie smiled sheepishly. "I always enjoyed washing the raisins for the Raisin Drop cookies," she recalled. "Only I ate half of the raisins while washing them!"

The women laughed, reminiscing on other baking experiences. The atmosphere became lighter with each story, reminding Rosie of the good times they had shared long ago.

Miriam sewed new dresses and choring aprons for her daughter. The dresses Rosie had left behind were thread-bare and far too small. However, to even think of wearing Miriam's matronly dresses would have been preposterous – she would have swum in them. So, while Miriam handstitched the clothing, Rosie concentrated on stitching new Prayer *kappes* and a bonnet. At times she became frustrated, especially after pricking her finger for the zillionth time. "Oww," Rosie groaned. "How could I ever forget how to sew? We were always sewing samplers and darning holes in socks."

"You'll get it," Miriam encouraged. "Remember the times you and your *schwesters* sewed dresses for your dolls? It's just sewing something a few sizes larger," Miriam smiled.

"I know I can do it, *Mamm*. It's just so discouraging because my left hand isn't very strong yet, and I get tired of holding the material." When they didn't meet her expectations, Rosie began pulling some of the stitches out of her work.

Miriam clucked disapprovingly at the thought of Rosie's abuse and leaned over to check her daughter's work. "Let me see how I can help."

"I'm sorry, *Mamm*. I'm not trying to be impatient. Maybe I should put it down and give my arm a rest," she folded her sewing neatly and set it in the sewing basket. They hugged each other, fighting back threatening tears.

"*Ja*. It's time I thought about supper. Why don't you go and rest your hands and face?"

Rosie smiled, "Your *Mamm* used to say that to you, didn't she?"

"*Ja*. I miss her." Miriam nodded, remembering. "We did so much together."

"Just like you and I are now," Rosie became the encouraging one.

"*Ja*. And we will for a long time to *kumme*." Miriam smiled at her daughter and pushed up from her chair. "Go and put your feet up. Seth will be up from his nap soon enough."

Occasionally Rosie and Esther sat by the pond's edge, swirling the water with their feet and chatting. Most of their chats rang with laughter, their voices carrying across the water's surface. No longer able to contain her curiosity, Esther finally asked:

"Why didn't you *kumme* home when things didn't work out?" Esther questioned her friend, trying to understand why anyone would stay in an abusive situation.

"Well, at first, it was okay between Dennis and me. But when I found out I was expecting Seth," Rosie smiled at her little boy and reached down to brush his hair back from his eyes. "I thought it would change everything. You know how we put family first – so, naturally, I thought he would be happy I was carrying his *boppli*. But he wasn't. After that, sometimes he'd hit me for no reason, especially when he'd been drinking."

"Then why didn't you *kumme* home?" Esther persisted.

Rosie shrugged and watched the water ripple in broader and broader circles away from her ankles. "I just thought it would get better – if today wasn't a *gut* day, then maybe tomorrow would be better."

A thoughtful "Hmm," escaped Esther, but she didn't understand why her friend would stay in such an unhealthy relationship. "Did you get married to him?"

"*Nee*," Rosie shook her head sadly. "I thought he would when I told him I was expecting, but he just laughed and said marriage was for weak people – that it's a crutch."

Esther didn't know how to respond. She remembered how she had felt when Thomas had been aloof and distant with her. She remembered thinking his attitude would improve once he had job security. Perhaps, that was what Rosie had hoped for – that things would get better. The hurtful memory was still very fresh, so Esther looped a comforting arm through Rosie's rather than saying anything to her friend, and they sat watching the swans dive for vegetation on the bottom of the pond.

Rosie's broad smile returned. Her blue eyes took on some of their former sparkle. As the days turned into weeks, Rosie's melancholy dissipated. The heartrending sadness that threatened to extinguish her joyful nature drifted aimlessly away, as did the pond's ripples. Rosie sat on the porch and took in the quiet night air in the evenings, reminiscing about spending similar moments with her parents and sisters. A look of endearment softened her facial features as she listened to her parent's conversation. She held Seth close while her foot gently rocked the chair, listening to her dad's report of the Mill. Once taken for granted, these were times that she now held dear. The continual unrest of the city no longer held sway over her. Rosie was only too glad to be home near the companionship and support of her parents. 'Why couldn't I have seen that before?' She mused, now seeing the security in her childhood home, knowing she need not fear anything. But, those years with Dennis had instilled a deep-seated dread within her - one that would be hard to overcome.

Rose often wandered in the garden, plucking juicy red raspberries from the canes drooping heavy with fruit. It had become a luxury for her to eat the fresh food straight from the garden. Seth experimented with gooseberries and raspberries, squishing them between baby fingers. His spontaneous broad smile, showing tiny white teeth stained red with berry juice, caused Rosie to laugh. It was a new experience for Seth to hear Rosie laugh, and he wasn't sure what to make of it. His smile turned to a scowl, but when Rosie tickled him, he squirmed at the unfamiliar sensation and began to giggle. It was the first time Rosie had ever heard him laugh – seeing him so happy brought tears flooding into her eyes.

While Rosie weeded in the garden, enclosed by fencing to keep the rabbits out, Seth waddled up and down the rows of vegetables. Nevertheless, she kept a protective eye on him, often searching for him since he had recently developed no fear of the outdoors. It was a new experience for the little boy to run unsupervised, chewing on baby carrots and string beans. Life for Seth was becoming an adventure. Rosie encouraged his newfound freedom, but she was forced to draw the line one day. Seth, digging in the dirt, uncovered an earthworm. She stood back, watching with an amused grin as Seth examined the wriggling worm.

When he lifted the squirming fishworm to his mouth, she called out, alarmed. "Seth, *nee!*" He looked at her and grinned. On baby legs, he toddled over to her with his prize. Taking pity on the poor worm, Rosie dug a hole in the garden and carefully sprinkled it over with earth. Seth stared at his disappearing worm, sat down abruptly, and opened his mouth, grief-stricken, protesting with a loud wail. Rosie gathered him in her arms and gently unearthed the worm. They looked at it together. "Now we need to cover him up so he can go to sleep," she explained. She gently helped him pat the soil over the squirmy creature by placing some earth in his hand. "*Kumme*," Rosie stood up, diverting Seth's attention. "*Dawdi* will be in for lunch soon."

Eager to see his grandfather, Seth hurried ahead of Rosie and waited at the garden gate.

Seth was a picky eater other than eating berries and trying to eat the earthworm. It took Miriam and Rosie's combined efforts to get him to eat. Often, he picked food from Tobiah's plate when he saw how his grandfather relished what was on it. No one corrected him; they were only too happy to see him showing an interest in food.

Tobiah dedicated hours to gaining Seth's trust. He didn't want the little boy to be traumatized when introduced to the other men in their community. Often, he carried his grandson to the barn to see a new batch of kittens or baby chicks. On other days, Tobiah toted him to the Mill while he talked with his men before they started work. One such day, Tobiah set Seth on the floor to play with some wooden blocks. He thought he was keeping a protective eye on the youngster while chatting with his men. Seconds later, turning to pick the youngster up, Tobiah's face drained of all color. The blocks were on the floor, but Seth was gone.

"Don't start up that blade!" Tobiah barked at his men. "Help me find my *enkel*." His eyes searched frantically about the mill, his mind racing, imagining the worst.

With twelve men searching for one little boy, it wasn't long before someone found him.

"He's over here playin' in the sawdust," a young man called and picked the little boy up, carrying him to Tobiah.

Seth scowled at the young man and struggled to get down.

"*Kumme*," Tobiah scooped the squirming child into his arms. "It's time I took ya back ta yer *Mamm*." He picked the wooden blocks up off the floor and minutes later handed everything, part, and parcel, over to Miriam and Rosie with a warning. "Keep an eye on him; he's as slippery as a greased pig."

Rosie, being forewarned, watched as Seth attempted to follow behind her dad. When Tobiah reached for his straw hat, Seth was ready to go. "Might be best if'n ya keep the screen door locked, or he'll be gone faster than a watermelon on a hot day," Tobiah chuckled, shaking his head as he securely closed the screen door on his way out.

Seth sat on the floor and howled, heartbroken when he wasn't allowed to go outside. Nothing Rosie or Miriam did could appease him; it was apparent that he was grandpa's boy.

Tobiah, returning home from the Mill each afternoon, was always met by his grandson, causing Tobiah to recall how Rosie had done the same thing when she was small. Without fail, Tobiah carried Seth to his bed at night, Rosie following close behind.

It amazed Rosie how it took the whole community to reconstruct the damage done by one. But, to everyone's relief, she was now home. The horrors of the previous three years became like a distant bad dream. Rosie's ready smile and the kindly sparkle in her blue eyes returned as she became more stable. She even lightened her overprotective ways with Seth. The sound of her soft voice and laughter lightened Miriam and Tobiah's heavy hearts - for now, they were a family again.

~ ~ ~

He restoreth my soul:
He leadeth me in paths of righteousness ...
~ Psalm 23: 3 ~

Chapter 4
A Price of Great Worth

Two months after returning home, Rosie was well enough and strong enough to attend her first Sunday Meeting with her parents. She knew most young adults her age, having gone to school with many young women like Esther, Naomi, and her sister Ruthie. There were also the other supportive women who'd been with her the last couple of months: her mother – of course, Eva, May, and Anna Woerner. For Rosie, it was akin to a huge family reunion.

After the Meeting and following the pot-luck luncheon, Rosie settled Seth in a makeshift play area to play with some other children. She knew it was important he socialized with children nearer his age. Watching him dig in a pile of sand, she stood near him, then turned to visit with Naomi, Esther, and her sister.

Esther reminded, "Have you given it any more thought helping *Mamm* and me make quilts to sell in the store in town? It would be a *wunderbar* way for you to make a little money on the side."

Rosie nodded thoughtfully. "*Ja*. Now that my arm is stronger, I need to do something - I don't want to be a burden on my folks forever."

"What do you want to work at?" Naomi asked, shifting her little one in her arms.

"Just about anything," Rosie shrugged.

Anna, overhearing the girls chatting, interrupted. "Would you like to clean *haus* once or twice a week?"

Rosie smiled at the woman who had been instrumental in helping nurse her back to health. "*Ja*. As long as I can take Seth with me." She glanced at her son, still playing in the sand with the other children.

"I have one or two places in mind. When could you start?"

"Well, since you're my *doctor*, when do you suggest?" Rosie returned, smiling.

"Light cleaning, like washing windows, a general tidy-up and dusting, right away - heavier work, such as washing clothes and scrubbing floors a little longer," Anna recommended.

"Then, if you know of anyone needing some help, I guess I'm ready." Rosie gave a typical Tobiah-like grin.

"I have a few places in mind, but let me check them out, and I'll get back to you." Anna smiled, turned, and walked away, deep in thought.

Rosie returned to the conversation with the other young women, glancing at Seth to confirm he was still near. Her friends, eager to catch up, talked over themselves, animated. Naomi and Ruthie's young babies were passed around the group as they chatted.

Miriam joined the young women and took her turn, holding her new grandchild. Leaning toward her daughter, she queried, "How are you enjoying the day, Rosie?"

"It's *gut* to see so many of my friends again."

Miriam nodded, pleased. "We'll leave in another half hour or so."

"*Ach*, is there anything I can do to help?"

"*Nee*. Just letting you know, is all." Miriam smiled, settling her grandchild in Ruthie's arms, then left to pack their dishes in the buggy.

While the young women continued chatting, catching up with new and old news, groups of men did the same thing. Hezekiah, Anna's son, exchanged views on farming with the other men. His attention was caught by the nervous sidestepping of some of the horses tied to the fence-line. Interested in what had the horses so uptight, he left the cluster of men. Striding over to the tethered horses, he patted one and then another, reassuring them. His heart jumped up to his throat. A small boy wandered through the horses, walking under bellies and patting legs. With a quickness that belied his size, Hezekiah sidled over to the older horse that the child was patting.

"Hi. How are ya?" He had no idea how to talk to children this young. Except for his brother Charles' little ones, he didn't know a thing about little kids.

The little boy looked up at him and gave a toothy grin.

"What's yer name?" He moved cautiously toward the child.

"Mama," the little boy smiled while pulling on the horse's leg hairs.

Hezekiah stooped to pick the child up and sighed with relief. "What's yer *Mamma's* name," he tried another approach.

"Mama," the child repeated.

"Ask a dumb question," Hezekiah muttered to himself. 'I can see we're goin' nowhere fast with this conversation,' he thought wryly. Settling the child up on his shoulders, he tried again. "Where's yer *Mamma*?" He looked about at the different groups of women for someone who might seem a little anxious.

"Mama," the boy held his hand out to a group of young women talking. Hezekiah recognized his sister, Naomi standing with Esther and Ruthie and someone else who looked too young to be this boy's mother.

"That's a dead-end, Buddy. I don't see yer *Mamma* there." Turning, he looked in the opposite direction. Relieved, he saw his mother walking toward him, smiling.

"Hezekiah, who do you have there?" Anna smiled up at Seth playfully.

"I don't know, he was walkin' under the horses, an' all I can get outa him is, *Mamma*. If I ask him his name, he says, *Mamma*. When I asked his Mamm's name, he says, *Mamma*."

"Mama," the little boy insisted, holding his hand out toward the group of young women, opening and closing his fingers.

Anna laughed. "Well, he does know who his *Mamm* is. *Kumme* with me," and she led the way toward Esther and Naomi.

Naomi was the first to see them coming and smiled at her brother. "Who did you find?"

"Nomi," Hezekiah addressed his sister. "My Buddy here insists that you or Esther is his *Mamm*."

"Mama," the child reached forward.

"Seth!" The young woman that had been talking with his sister exclaimed. "What are you doing up there?"

Hezekiah explained without elaborating. He didn't want to frighten this young mother. "He was over walkin' near the horses, so I redirected him a little."

"I left him over playing with the other *kinder*." She turned to look behind her as if expecting to see him still there. "I guess he must have gone exploring." Rosie looked up at her son, shaking her head. A broad smile of love and relief covered her face when she saw he was alright.

"Rosie?" Hezekiah asked hesitantly, recognizing her as soon as she smiled. 'She sure looks awful thin,' he realized, suddenly concerned.

"*Ja*," Rosie looked long and hard at the man who rescued her son. "Hezekiah?"

"*Ja*," he nodded. When he realized he was staring, Hezekiah lifted the child from his shoulders and handed him to Rosie. "It's *gut* ta see ya," he stammered. "An' it's *gut* ta have found his *Mamm*."

"*Danke*. I'm glad you found him before he got into any trouble." Rosie smiled at Seth while balancing him on her hip.

"*Ja*. Me too," Hezekiah added, realizing how close the little fellow had come to being seriously injured. "I'm glad ta help." As an afterthought added, "An' it's *gut* ta see ya again." He nodded toward the ladies before turning and walking back to the group of men still talking about farming.

Anna watched the exchange between her son and Tobiah's daughter. If she wasn't mistaken, there was a connection between the two, somehow and someway. Putting two and two together, she realized they must have known each other in school. She squinted in contemplation.

Shortly after rejoining the men, Hezekiah left the huddle, no longer interested in farm talk. All he could think about was Rosie and her little boy. Disappointed, that meant that she had a husband somewhere, but Hezekiah hadn't noticed any new faces. Then again, he'd missed seeing Rosie until handing over the little boy. He supposed it would be only neighborly to welcome him, whoever he was, so he mingled, intent on keeping an eye out for this new man's face. A half-hour later, Hezekiah gave up looking. Frustrated, he went to the horses tied at the fence, retrieved his horse, and led him to the buggy.

"Hezekiah," Anna hurried over. "Are you leaving already?"

"*Ja*. I need ta get home ta feed the calves," he answered, distracted, still wondering who had married Rosie.

"I have someone who can *kumme* to do a little *hauswork* for you."

He stopped what he was doing and looked at his mother, confused. "I thought ya looked after the *haus* fer me?"

"I said I could until I got too busy. It seems there are more *bopplies* on the way. As it is, I'll be going in all different directions at once. I hope you don't mind?"

"*Ja, Mamm*," Hezekiah shrugged. "Whatever ya thinks best," he muttered as he pulled the buggy up to the waiting horse.

"I'd like to bring her over and show her around your *haus*." Anna hastened before her son drove off. "Are Wednesday's *gut* when you take the veal calves to the Stockyards in Kitchener?"

"*Ja.* Just whenever is *gut* fer ya an' her," he climbed into the buggy. "I'll leave some money on the counter fer her?"

"Maybe it would be better to put it in the breadbox."

"*Danke, Mamm*," he smiled at his mother and clucked to the horse. His drive home was preoccupied with thoughts of the happy little girl he'd once known and the woman she had become.

Anna gave a deflated sigh and turned back toward the different gatherings of people. Beckoning Rosie, she said, "I'm looking after a *haus* that needs light work done each week. Would you be interested in taking it over for me? I could pick you up Wednesday morning to show you around."

Rosie smiled. "*Ach, danke.* This way, I can help *Mamm* and *Dat* out with our expenses. Where is the *haus*?"

"You probably won't remember the place, but it's only a couple of lines over from your place. I can pick you up around nine Wednesday morning?"

"*Ja*, that's a *gut* time." Rosie smiled. "What are their names?" She asked, thinking it was probably an older couple needing a little help.

Anna returned Rosie's smile. "*Ach*, it's just an *alt*, confirmed bachelor that's recently moved back to the area," she brushed aside the question. At Rosie's scowl, Anna hastily added, "There's no need for concern. He never married and is set in his ways."

"And it's alright that I take Seth?"

"Not to worry. He's always away on Wednesdays, so you'll have the whole *haus* to yourself. I'll pick you up Wednesday morning - you and Seth."

"*Danke,* Anna." Rosie grinned happily. "*Danke* for everything."

"*Nee. Danke* to you. I've been looking for someone to take this *haus* off my hands for a long time." At Rosie's confused frown, she enlightened. "I've been cleaning it every week, but I'm getting too busy with new *Mamm's* and soon-to-be new *Mamm's*."

Rosie nodded in understanding. "Seth and I will be ready when you come for us."

"*Gut.* Let me know when you think you're ready for more work."

"I will," Rosie promised and went looking for her parents. Seth was beginning to get fussy, and she knew if she didn't get him home for a rest, it would soon be too late to lay him down.

Rosie filled her parents in on the job prospects on the drive home. They nodded with approval at helping Esther and Eva with quilting. When she told them of the housekeeping job, her parents immediately scowled and became defensive.

"Where is this place?" Tobiah prodded.

"I'm not sure. Anna says it's only a couple of lines from our place."

"How does Anna know about this job?" Miriam asked.

"She's doing the cleaning there right now, but she's getting too busy with new *Mamm's* and more *bopplies* on the way. So, she asked me if I'd take the *haus* over. She's going to take Seth and me over Wednesday morning."

"So, Anna's takin' ya over?" Tobiah asked, getting his facts straight.

"*Ja*. That way, I can help you and *Mamm* with expenses."

"There's no need for that," Tobiah protested.

"But I want to. You and *Mamm* have done so much for me as it is."

"But ain't that what families are fer? Ta help one another?" Tobiah asked.

"*Ja*. And if Seth and I are to be part of this family, it's only right that I help. In this way, I can help – even if it's only a little."

"*Das gut*," Tobiah shrugged begrudgingly. "I know we'd feel the same way, and I don't know too many Amish freeloaders. Just don't overdo it," he cautioned. "It's only been a few short weeks since..." he mumbled, leaving the sentence unfinished.

Rosie and Seth were waiting Wednesday morning after receiving her parents' blessing. As promised, Anna picked them up at nine. Rosie looked about them as Anna chatted and drove the horse. Breathing in the fresh morning air was invigorating. It was sharp with frost; a sign summer was coming to an end and fall was around the corner. Chasing fast on its heels would come snowy winter winds.

Anna pulled into a drive overgrown with weeds and unpruned shrubs. They rounded a stand of trees, and an old clapboard house came into view. Dry leaves on the paper birch rustled in the slight breeze. The siding on the house had been painted white at one time, but now it was faded and peeling.

"*Ach*," Rosie, overwhelmed, looked at the condition of the outside of the house and the yard.

"The inside is better," Anna assured her. "As I said, he hasn't been in the area very long and is cleaning it up when he gets time. The barn took priority, so the stock was protected, and he needed a place to store feed for the animals."

Rosie stayed quiet but nodded her head in understanding.

After bringing the horse to a stop at a hitching post, Anna climbed out of the buggy. Rosie carried Seth as they walked up a worn path to the house. The porch housed two chairs, waiting for someone to come and sit in them when it was too hot to spend evenings inside. Rosie watched as Anna turned the knob to the unlocked door and followed her inside, entering an area that was obviously the kitchen. There were dishes in the sink and on the counter, and a blackened woodstove still had a dirty pot sitting on it. In general, the house screamed to be looked after; in addition to other care, it was in dire need of a woman's touch. Anna showed Rosie through the house, pointing out the cleaning supplies in the hall closet.

"I usually start in the kitchen. It's the area most lived in, then I go through the whole *haus*, and whatever I can get done in two hours, I get done. Otherwise," Anna raised her shoulders in a shrug. "It doesn't get done, unfortunately."

"Is that all I can stay - two hours?" Rosie asked, disappointed.

"*Nee.* You can stay longer, but that's all the time I could spare. Remember, don't overdo it until you build up your strength. You've been through a lot." She raised her eyebrows at Rosie. "And I don't want to answer to your *Mamm* if you get hurt again."

"*Ja.* You're right. Slow and easy wins the race. Ain't?"

Anna smiled at her young charge. She liked her. Rosie had backbone, and she was a sweet girl. But she had just gone down the wrong path, like many of their young people. What was important was that she was back. "*Kumme.* Together we'll put the *haus* to rights, then do you think you can manage it after that?"

"*Ja.* I know I can," Rosie looked around the kitchen. 'It's a big improvement over where I lived before *Daed* came for us.'

With a concentrated effort, she thrust the ugliness of the years with Dennis aside. 'You have a new life here, where people care about you.' Encouraged, she embraced what was before her.

Two hours later, the cleaning and tidying behind them, Rosie and Anna, stood in the kitchen. Everything looked good, and it smelled clean.

"Now, if only it could stay this way," Anna joked, satisfied with their job.

"When I *kumme* each week, maybe I could do one more thing, like scrub the floor or wash windows," Rosie envisioned.

"I'll try to find time to ask him to tidy after himself, and then you can." Anna smiled. "It's time to leave. I don't want you overdoing it for a little while, and I need to get home." They closed the door and went out to the waiting horse. Rosie looked about the yard. 'One more area to tackle,' she determined and put it on her mental to-do list.

That night, Rosie slept well. Not a sleep of exhaustion, but one of feeling secure and of a job well done. She looked forward to Esther's invitation to join her in quilting the next day. It was something she could hardly wait to do. Eventually, Rosie planned on making a quilt for Seth's bed and one for herself. Life had new promises, and she intended to savor each one. God had given her another chance at life - an opportunity she'd once taken for granted; now, she saw beauty in all things. She was indeed Tobiah and Miriam's daughter, perpetually looking at everything optimistically. Her name, Rosie, suited her well.

~ ~ ~

... the unfading beauty of a gentle and quiet spirit,
Is of great worth in God's sight
~ 1 Peter 3:4 ~

Chapter 5
Honest Provision

Rosie glanced out the kitchen window, amused, noticing how the wind played with the leaves in the yard. The gusts of wind blew more leaves off the trees. She watched, fascinated, as they drifted lazily down, nestling with those already blanketing the ground. "It looks windy out there."

"*Ja*. It'll hurry fall along, fer sure," Tobiah commented. "Are ya goin' out this mornin'?" He looked over his shoulder at his daughter as he finished washing at the kitchen pump.

"*Ja*. I'm going to my *hauskeeping* job after I help *Mamm* in the kitchen."

"I'll get the horse ready fer ya. Eight o'clock, *gut*?"

"*Ja*. That'll give me a chance to get Seth's things ready and freshen up before leaving."

As she carried breakfast to the table, Miriam added, "Make sure you use that lilac-chamomile soap I made up in the spring. I want to use it up, so we can make another batch more suited to fall."

"*Danke, Mamm*. It's always been my favorite."

"Mine too," Tobiah winked at Miriam.

"*Ach*, you. Just go sit down," Miriam flustered, but her heightened color indicated Tobiah's words had been flattering.

Later, Rosie splashed quickly in the tub, longing to linger, but that wasn't a luxury appointed her this morning. Lathering her body generously with the bar of lilac-chamomile soap, she considered, 'It seems rather redundant, getting a bath before I get dirty cleaning *haus*.' She shrugged her shoulders and rinsed away the soapsuds. While she slid into her clothes, she wondered for the umpteenth time what this old bachelor was like. 'One thing,' she concluded, 'He's not much at keeping *haus*. But then again, I wouldn't have a job if he was.' She placed her Prayer *kappe* on her head and hurried down the steps.

"I packed a snack for you and Seth if you get hungry," Miriam informed. "We'll have soup and sandwiches when you get home for lunch."

"*Danke, Mamm*. That'll give me three to three and a half hours to clean the *haus* and do a few extras."

"Don't go overdoing it." Miriam cautioned, reminding her, "Last week, you didn't get to Esther's because you had overdone it helping Anna with the *haus*."

"I'll try not to, *Mamm*, but I was hoping to get the kitchen windows done before stopping."

Miriam just shook her head. "Here's your *daed* with the horse. I'll carry Seth if you can take the bag with your snack and his things."

While Rosie was helping her mother in the kitchen and later getting organized to go to her job, a cattle truck rattled up the drive to Hezekiah's farm. Twenty-five veal calves were ushered up the high-sided ramp into the transport trailer and were soon on their way to the Stockyard in Kitchener. Hezekiah and his dad, passengers in a van they had hired, followed the livestock truck, arriving in plenty of time for Hezekiah to settle the calves before the auctioning began.

~ ~ ~

Two years earlier, Hezekiah had returned home after being away a year and a half. Immediately upon returning home, he had a job working on Eli Kuepfer's dairy farm. In his free time, he scouted the countryside, looking for a farm suitable to begin his own business - raising veal calves. Unsuccessful in finding a farm without spending hundreds of thousands of dollars, he and his dad recruited Tobiah Yoder in the search. Taking Tobiah's advice, they investigated a farm on the verge of being auctioned off for back taxes. By buying the farm from the owner and paying the back taxes, both Woerner men knew they had made a good investment, as far as the land value went, but the house and the barn were in dire need of attention. Tobiah came to the rescue again, repairing the barn's roof and replacing the shingles on the house. Hezekiah and his dad decided they could handle all other repairs over time to save money.

At the age of twenty-three, Hezekiah Woerner began his veal calf operation. He bought bull calves from nearby dairy farms and fed and fattened them for the market in eighteen weeks. After selling his first lot of calves, Hezekiah, frugal with his money, began repaying his dad for the down payment on the farm. He bought another group of calves, kept a small percentage for living expenses, paid ten percent tithe on the money he'd cleared, and placed twenty-five percent into savings. By working hard for two years, his dividends began to show the fruits of his labor, and he began rotating his calves. When the first twenty-five were ready for market, the next group was already half-grown. The turnover was lucrative; before long, the farm was well on its way to being paid off and the business established.

Once the calves were sold and the money deposited in the bank where Hezekiah had gotten a loan to buy the farm, the Woerner men returned to the farm.

"Guess ya can breathe fer a spell," Charles assumed.

Hezekiah chuckled, "*Nee*. I have stalls ta clean out an' disinfect, then move this lot over ta the larger pens. Once I clean out an' disinfect the smaller pens, I'll make my rounds of the different farms ta pick up the calves they've been keepin' fer me. If'n I can't find twenty-five calves, I'll have ta look further afield or go back ta Kitchener ta fill my quota."

"If'n ya need ta go, let me know, an' I'll go with ya," his dad offered.

"*Ja. Danke Dat.* I will." Hezekiah nodded.

"Yer doin' a real *gut* job. Before ya know it, you'll have a nice little savin's put away," Charles encouraged. "Ya can start fixin' the *haus*, even put up some fencin'." He hesitated before adding, "Maybe ya could find a *frau* an' start a family. That way ya'd have *kinder* ta pass the business on ta."

Hezekiah became quiet, uncomfortable talking about marriage with his dad. He changed the topic to break the deafening silence that had suddenly grown between them. "I saw Rosie Yoder at Meetin' the other day. I went lookin' fer her *mann* ta say, *willkommen*, but I didn't see any new faces."

"*Nee*, an' ya won't either. She ain't got one," Charles became reserved, and a firmness settled around his mouth.

"But she has a *boppli;* there must be one somewhere," Hezekiah insisted, frowning at his dad.

Charles looked at his son, eyes squinting in contemplation. "Not necessarily. Not in this day an' age," he muttered. "I'll tell ya somethin', but it's confidential. An' what I'm tellin' ya, I know 'cause Jed's shirt was covered in blood when he came ta get yer *Mamm's* help."

Hezekiah stood up a little straighter, peering closely at his dad. It wasn't like his dad to pass rumors or gossip.

"When Rosie was on *rumspringa,* she got mixed up with some *Englischer*. From what yer *Mamm* says, he held her against her will, beat her, an' did what he wanted with her. Somehow, she was able ta leave a message askin' Tobiah ta *kumme* an' get her. Said she couldn't look after her *boppli* with a broken arm." Charles didn't notice Hezekiah's sudden stricken look and went on. "Tobiah went an' got the boy, but the *Englischer* wouldn't let her go. So, the next day Tobiah went back fer her. This guy had beat her an' left her fer dead. Tobiah had ta break the door down when he went back. He found her unconscious, layin' in a pool of blood, an' a newborn *boppli* layin' dead beside her. Tobiah only got her out in time. So, *nee,* she ain't got no *mann.* An' if'n he knows what's *gut* fer him, he won't show up here, either. 'Cause, there's men here that don't put up with that nonsense of poundin' on womenfolk. An' I'm one of them."

Hezekiah turned away; the shock of hearing what Rosie had been through caused all color to drain from his face. "He did that ta Rosie? My Rosie," he choked, a great shudder shaking his shoulders.

Surprised by his son's words and reaction, Charles attempted to amend, "She's safe here with us now. Is it any wonder why we worry when our *kinder* go away on *rumspringa*? They have no idea what dangers they can *kumme* up against in the *Englischer* world."

While Hezekiah attempted to come to grips with his dad's news, Charles cleared his throat. "I shouldn't be tellin' ya all this, an' if'n yer *Mamm* knew, she'd kill me fer sure."

Hezekiah glanced at his dad, thinking he was exaggerating. 'There's no way *Mamm* could kill *Dat*. He's a big solid *mann*!' It struck him as funny the thought of his mom putting his dad in line, and a smirk lifted the corners of his mouth.

"It's no laughin' matter. Don't ya breathe a word about any of this," Charles insisted, looking worried.

Hezekiah had no intention of starting a family feud and shook his head as if to clear it. 'All this drama goin' on, right under my nose, an' I had no idea.' "Don't worry, *Dat*," he assured. "Nobody would believe me anyway, except maybe *Mamm,* an' I ain't goin' ta be the one ta see ya get killed by her. *Kumme*," he beckoned. "I'll help ya catch up yer horse so's ya can get home on time fer supper." He laughed lightly, amused. "I wouldn't like ta see *Mamm* kill ya 'cause ya was late."

Charles gave his son a withering look but followed him to catch the horse from the field, harness him, and put him into the buggy. "Let me know when yer goin' fer that new lot of calves, an' I'll help ya out. It'll go faster with the two of us workin' tagether."

"*Ja.* Give me a couple of days, and then I'll swing around yer way."

They bid one another goodbye. While Charles drove out the drive, Hezekiah headed to the house thinking. 'So, Rosie

never got married.' He pushed open the door to the kitchen.
A slow smile lifted the corners of his mouth as he looked at
the neatness of the kitchen and clean windows. His brows
pulled together in contemplation. 'That smell - nice and
fresh like early spring blowing through an open window.'
He glanced at the window – it was closed; furthermore, it
was well past spring. In fact, summer was behind them, and
the fall weather was fast approaching. He inhaled deeply,
but as hard as he tried, he couldn't remember where he'd
smelled that fresh scent of spring. Finally, he gave up trying
to place the pleasing fragrance and concluded, '*Ja*. I'd say
havin' someone *kumme* ta clean every week is *gut* – real *gut*.
He turned to go back outside. Closing the door, Hezekiah
noticed the garden under the kitchen window had been
weeded. He nodded in satisfaction, concluding this was
where the fresh, outdoors perfume must be coming. A
pleased smile lifted the corners of his mouth as he headed
toward the barn and the chore that awaited him. 'Now, if
only there was a way to take that fresh, clean smell with
me,' he chuckled.

Rosie walked slowly up the Kuepfer lane the following
morning, keeping in step with Seth's shorter strides. Often,
they stopped to examine the blue flower on the chickweed
or the fluffy seeds exploding out of the milkweed plant.
They were on their way to see how Esther and Eva worked
on quilt blocks. Esther had been very convincing.
"Quilting in this fashion is so much easier. Much easier
than trying to keep one huge piece of material organized.
Smaller sampler pieces of material can go with you
wherever you go. That's the secret of *Mamm* and me

getting so many quilts finished to sell in town. And they do sell faster than we can make them," Esther assured.

Tapping lightly on the screen door, Rosie smiled broadly as her friend answered the door.

Full of enthusiasm, Esther threw open the door. "*Kumme* in Rosie. I've set some colors out on the table, and I'll show you how we learned to sew a quilt faster. I thought for our project today, we could use a tulip applique or one with the silhouette of a little girl picking flowers in her garden. It should get you started and work up real quick." Esther smiled broadly, happy to share her knowledge with her friend.

Looking at both samples, Rosie contemplated the patterns, unsure of the choice she needed to make. "*Ach,* they're both so pretty. But the little girl picking flowers with the oversized bonnet would be nice."

"*Ja.* I'm partial to that one too. First, we'll cut the material for each square. For this project, no two appliques should look alike. Each square with an applique sewn on it will alternate with a square of a solid color." She unfolded a small quilt so that Rosie could see an example. "You'll see here all the squares are sewn separately. Then, they are joined together with bands in a complementary color. Finally, we baste a quilt bat between the backing and the front, and once that's done, the whole quilt is whip stitched to a quilting frame."

At Rosie's look of excited eagerness, Esther laughed. "Let's take it one step at a time; there will be a quilt already sewn before you know it. We'll all work on it to get it finished. *Mamm* said it's only fair that we give you one-third the price of each quilt you sew, and that'll be splitting the price of the quilt three ways."

"Really? Are you sure you want to split the money in three ways? You are providing all the material."

"It's an easy enough project but time-consuming. And, it's more than fair. We may be supplying the material, but you're doing the work," Esther reminded with a smile and became businesslike. "Let's get the appliques cut out, and then we can start by turning the edges. You can take everything home, and when you're finished, bring them back, and we'll join them together into a quilt."

They sat at the kitchen table and cut out the appliques and squares. While talking about the quilt with Rosie, occasionally Esther peered at Seth, playing quietly on the kitchen floor with some wooden blocks. Finally, rising, she asked, "Would you like tea or *kaffee*?"

"*Ach*. I'd *willkommen* a cup of tea," Rosie glanced up, working without faltering until she had completed one square.

Esther looked over at her friend's work. "This is *gut*. The more you work at it, the easier it'll *kumme*." Tea finished, they packed all the material in a bag to make it easier for Rosie to carry. "I'll walk out with you," Esther offered. "Next time I go to the fabric store in town, I'll take you, and we can pick out material together." They walked down the lane, chatting as they went.

Rosie sighed happily as she and Seth made their way to her parents. Esther was such a good friend to have. Of all the things she missed the most while away from home was the companionship of family and friends.

Guiding Seth, Rosie climbed the two steps, one at a time to the back porch. Once inside, she pulled the sewing project out of the bag to show her mother.

"*Ach*, Ruthie would like to see this! I'm going over there this afternoon. Do you want to *kumme*?" Miriam offered after admiring the work Rosie had already accomplished.

Rosie shook her head. "Not this time, Mamm. Seth gets really cranky if he doesn't have his afternoon rest."

Miriam nodded her head in understanding. While they got lunch ready, she suggested. "Don't be overdoing it. You had your *hauskeeping* job yesterday, now making the quilt today and what you do around here. On top of that, you have Seth."

"*Ach, Mamm*. Seth is not hard to look after. I'd do anything for him."

"I don't want to see you are overdoing it, is all. I care about you the same as you care about him."

"*Ja*. I can see your point," Rosie nodded in contemplation. "I'll rest when he does. Like your *Mamm* said…"

"…sit down and rest your hands and face," Miriam finished. While prepping a tomato before slicing it, she emphasized, "Just don't go overdoing it."

"I won't, *Mamm*," Rosie assured while cutting the bread and setting it on the table.

That afternoon while Seth rested, Rosie completed another square. Soon, her eyes became heavy, so she closed them to rest, heeding her mother's counsel. She must have fallen asleep because she woke with a kink in her neck. Massaging it helped a little, but the cramp quickly became a muscle spasm. 'I suppose I have been overdoing it a little,' she sighed. Going to the bathroom, Rosie soaked a small towel in hot water. She squeezed out the excess water and placed the moist warm cloth on her neck. Minutes later, she replaced the hot compress with a cold towel. By the time Seth woke up, the neck spasm had disappeared, but Rosie realized she had been expecting a lot of her body of late and promised herself she'd slow down a little.

~ ~ ~

Providing for honest things,
not only in the sight of the Lord,
but also in the sight of men
~ 2 Corinthians 8:21 ~

Chapter 6
The Lord Strengthens

Friday morning, while tidying breakfast away, Miriam kept glancing at Rosie. She seemed unusually quiet and wondered if Rosie was pushing the limits with all she had taken on. She voiced her concern, "You've had a busy week; you aren't finding the workload too heavy, are you, Rosie?"

"*Nee*. I'm fine, *Mamma*. Just thinking about things is all," her voice petered off as she stared out the window at the mini whirlwind of leaves. Without turning, she asked in a lost, sad voice. "Once I put Seth down for his rest, would you keep an eye on him, *Mamm*?"

"For certain," Miriam assured.

"Do you mind if I take the driver out for an hour or so?"

"Are you running an errand?" Miriam asked, concerned.

"I just want to visit the cemetery before the weather changes." Rosie's eyes clouded with tears, and she gulped; it came across as a strangled moan.

Miriam wrapped her maternal arms around her daughter. "Do you want company?"

Rosie shook her head, comforted by her mother's words of concern. "*Nee*. I'll be alright, *Mamm*."

"Then bundle warm. There's a nor' easter blowing in, and it'll probably bring Fall with it.' Attempting to change the mood, Miriam added, "Soon, we'll have to start the canning."

"Okay, *Mamm*. I'll take a sweater," Rosie looked out the window as the wind blew leaves around the yard and smiled wanly. "I'm looking forward to helping with the canning."

"I generally exchange canned goods with Eva and May; it saves one person doing it all."

Rosie looked at her mother with a puzzled frown.

Miriam relieved Rosie was showing interest, explained. "I'll put down the applesauce, and they'll preserve the plums. Then we split them, so each family gets half."

"That must save a lot of work for one person," Rosie brightened.

"*Ja*. It seems to work out well for us. It might not be how most people do things, but we aren't most people." Miriam smiled.

"*Nee*. You aren't because you're special." Rosie gave a weak smile.

"Just like you're special to us. I'm so glad you're home with us." Miriam dashed away a tear.

"Me too, *Mamm*. Me too."

After lunch, Rosie carried a sleepy Seth up the stairs.

Before she disappeared upstairs, Miriam called after her. "I'm going to check the mail before you leave. I'll be back in five minutes or so."

"Okay, *Mamm*," Rosie called over her shoulder and continued climbing the steps.

Miriam hurried to the Mill, hunting up Tobiah to inform him. "Rosie asked me to keep an eye on Seth because she's going to the cemetery this afternoon. You wouldn't have a reason to be out that way, would you?"

"I can make one," Tobiah looked at his wife and read between the lines. They hadn't been married for more than twenty-five years to not be able to know what the other was thinking. "I'll stop by an' make sure she's alright."

"*Gut*. I need to get the mail and hurry back to the *haus*. Rosie is putting Seth down for his afternoon rest." Miriam hurried out of the Mill office as quickly as she had breezed in.

Within minutes, Rosie headed out the drive, the wind whipping the horse's tail about its back legs. 'I'm glad the horse isn't skittish,' she thought. 'A younger horse would be all over the road on a day like today.' Rosie clucked to the horse, asking him to trot. She wanted to say goodbye to her little girl before winter set in. Unbidden, tears coursed down her cheeks. She wiped them away and sniffed. 'It wouldn't do to go in the wrong direction because I'm not paying attention.'

Rosie pulled the horse up to a stout hitching rail outside the cemetery and walked slowly and reverently between the markers. Some were old and weather-worn, listing precariously, moss clinging to their chipped and faded finishes. A testimony of the years they had stood sentinel over the person resting there. Finally, standing before the tiny grave, so recent the grass hadn't yet fully grown over the little mound, Rosie's emotions overwhelmed her, and she fell to her knees and wept. Moments later, she felt more than heard someone kneel beside her. She glanced over, and Tobiah pulled her into his arms.

"If I'd only listened to you, *Dat*, none of this would have happened," she sobbed against his shirt.

"I blame myself that you left. None of this would have happened if I hadn't been so unreasonable." Tobiah's throat was thick with emotions.

"But then I wouldn't have Seth," she looked at him with puffy eyes.

"It's like a tumultuous river." Tobiah agreed. "Ya can't have one without the other."

Rosie nodded her head. "It may have been tumultuous, but now that river has turned to peace. In here," she held her hand over her chest. "I'm so glad to be home with you and *Mamm*. A place where Seth can grow up without fear. That wasn't a *gut* place for him, *Dat*."

"It wasn't a *gut* place fer ya either, Rosie girl. Now yer home, you'll get stronger. I know. *Gott* has a plan fer ya. I only wish ya woulda called me sooner."

"I couldn't. He never let me out of his sight; I guess he knew I'd leave if I ever got the chance."

"Then how did ya get a chance ta leave a message fer me?"

"Wanda, the lady next door had a phone put in, and she let me use it to call you. But he walked in without knocking, and I had to let on Seth had knocked the receiver off its cradle."

"Well, it was enough. *Kumme*," he helped her to her feet. "The weather is turnin' an' yer *Mamm* will be worried." Tobiah helped her climb up to the buggy seat, unwrapped the horse's rope from the hitching post, and followed her home.

The days that followed were crammed with canning preserves. A break came from the blustery fall winds.

"The *Englischers* call it Indian Summer, although I'll never know where they got that name from," Tobiah shook his head. "Regardless, it's *gut* ta get a break in the weather. We have a barn raisin' *kummin'* up, an' it's not much fun raisin' a barn when it's cold an' windy."

"A barn raising?" Miriam responded, all smiles. "Looks like we'll be busy baking," she smiled at Rosie. "We could bake up some pies and sweetbreads."

"I'd like to make potato salad," Rosie volunteered with a broad smile.

"*Ach*. One of the plus sides ta a barn raisin' - all that *gut* food." Tobiah sighed with exaggeration, bordering on contentment.

Miriam and Rosie laughed. "You aren't the only one looking forward to that," Miriam chuckled and turned back to finish putting the supper on the table.

"It makes one wonder if that's why everyone *kummes* out?" Rosie continued smiling.

The jovial attitudes at a barn raising made it more like a party atmosphere – Amish style. It was the only time other than Sunday Meetings when everyone got together. It was a time to join forces and help a neighbor in need.

The morning of the barn raising began bright and crisp. Dew that had rolled in from the Great Lakes had frozen on the blades of grass, making it crunch when anyone walked on it. As the horses trotted toward the building site, their breath puffed out great foggy configurations. There was an unmistakable air of excitement as the men gathered at the foundation of the future barn. The women would come later with baskets of bounty, setting them on makeshift tables.

~ ~ ~

The Lord is faithful,
He will strengthen you
And protect you
~ 2 Thessalonians 3:3 ~

Chapter 7
The Depths of the Sea

While Miriam guided their horse to the construction site, Rosie had her hands full, containing an energetic Seth. He wiggled out of her clasp and sat on the buggy floor only to stand up and hold onto the leather seat.

"I wish I had a little harness for him," Rosie sighed. "My arms get tired holding him all the time."

"There should be some young girls that can spell you off and if you can't find someone, let me know, and I'll watch him for a little while. Your *daed* will be busy supervising the work crews, or he would take a turn looking after Seth. I know he would."

"I suppose I should have stayed home," Rosie sighed, disheartened.

"Nonsense!" Miriam brushed her daughters' concerns aside. "Everybody *kummes* to barn raisings. We'll get along fine. But knowing how quick he is at disappearing - we need to take extra precautions." Miriam turned their driver into the lane leading up to the construction site.

When they arrived at the building site, they were met by young men assigned to meet incoming buggies. Some helped carry food to the waiting tables; others led horses away and settled them with hay and water. Their help was a blessing; it saved Rosie from dealing with Seth and carrying the food. 'One less worry,' Rosie thought and smiled, joining her sister, Ruthie, and friends Esther and

Naomi. "There's a *gut* turn out, ain't so?" She gazed about her.

"*Ja*, and still more *kumming*," Esther looked toward the road. She turned back to Rosie, "I'm glad you're here. How are you making out with the quilting squares?"

"Almost done," Rosie beamed. "Soon, I'll be *kumming* over, so you can help me with the next step."

Rosie and Esther began unpacking their baskets containing the food items. "*Ja, kumme* whenever you're ready," Esther encouraged with a smile before carrying a casserole to the kitchen to keep it warm on the stove.

Just before lunch, Miriam came over to the group of friends. "Will you girls clear away the dishes once they empty of food? Just set the empty plates and bowls under the table, and some of the other women will keep the food *kumming*. Rosie, I'll get you to look after the salads. Esther, I'll ask you to keep an eye on the table with casseroles. Ruthie can keep the salads *kumming*, and I'll bring out the hot casseroles as needed."

The young women nodded their understanding. This rotation system wasn't new to them – it was a system they used every Meeting Sunday. Quickly, they organized the food on their tables, ensuring there were enough serving utensils. Once the men descended on the buffet feast, the women would be kept busy keeping the tables stocked.

At lunchtime, the men came in shifts. The last group was slowly making their way down the row of tables laden with food. Rosie held fast to Seth and smiled as her dad shifted with the line of men until he faced her from across the table.

"How's the building *kumming, Dat*?"

"Right on schedule, Rosie girl. It's a *gut* turn out, ain't?"

Rosie smiled at her dad. "*Ja*. Many hands make light work."

"*Ja*. An' eat a lot of food, too," he chuckled and continued adding food to his plate.

Seth's insistent, "Mama. Mama," interrupted Rosie's response. Looking at him, puzzled, she wondered what was wrong. It was certain his attention was captive because he kept calling, "Mama, Mama." He leaned away from her, opening and closing his tiny fists. Rosie followed the direction of his gaze. Hezekiah made his way down the table, placing food on his plate. Rosie looked at Seth; he was definitely focusing on Hezekiah.

"Mama," he began smiling a broad toothy grin as Hezekiah drew closer.

"That's Hezekiah," Rosie attempted to correct him.

"Mama," Seth insisted.

Hezekiah heard Seth and lifted his eyes from the vast selection of food. Smiling at the little boy, he chuckled, "Well, I've been called a lot of things in my lifetime, but that's a first," he laughed outright. Setting his plate on the table, he reached across the food at Seth's, demanding, "Mama."

"I'll take him for a spell, Rosie. Ya look busy here." He perched the little boy on his shoulders and picked up his plate. Hezekiah paused for a moment. "Ya don't mind if'n I take him while I eat, do ya, Rosie? I'll bring him back before we start buildin' again."

"Are you sure?" Rosie questioned.

"Absolutely. We don't want ta disappoint the little guy, do we?"

"*Nee*, I suppose not." Rosie, flabbergasted, hurriedly asked, "What do you want to drink? I'll bring it over for you."

"Lemonade would be *gut, danke*."

Rosie watched him make his way over to sit at the table beside his dad, across the table from her dad and Jed Kuepfer. She took a break from her table duties to take the lemonade to Hezekiah.

"Are ya not goin' ta get the rest of us a drink, Rosie girl? Or is Hezekiah the only one that gets preferred treatment?" Tobiah's booming voice questioned.

Rosie and Hezekiah blushed at her dad's remark while the other men sitting at the table attempted to squelch amused chuckles.

"I'll be right back, *Dat*," Rosie hurried away for a pitcher of lemonade and three more glasses.

Sometime later, Hezekiah carried Seth back to Rosie. "He won't be hungry 'cause he helped me eat my lunch."

"Really? He's usually a picky eater."

"Well, not taday. It's probably the fresh air. He'll most likely have a nap. He kept yawning." Hezekiah informed her.

"*Ja*. It's about that time of day," Rosie returned, examining Seth's heavy eyes. "*Danke* for looking after him. My arms were getting tired of holding him."

"No trouble," he assured her. "After all, it's not every day *kinder* calls a *mann, Mamma*. Wouldn't want ta disappoint the little fella," he smiled, laughter in his eyes as he settled Seth in her arms.

Rosie, looking up at him, returned his smile. 'Funny, I never thought of Hezekiah as a handsome *mann*.'

Mentally, she shook her head. 'Where did that thought *kumme* from – way out in the left field, that's for sure.' "Well, *danke*. You're very kind. Most men wouldn't look at it that way."

"Then again, I ain't most men. Am I Rosie? Or hadn't ya noticed?" He looked into her startled eyes. Sobering, a frown knitted his brow as he inhaled. 'There it is again - that fragrance of spring.'

Rosie saw Hezekiah's eyebrows shoot up, staring at her in disbelief. Inhaling a deep gasp of air, he seemed to stand taller, stepping suddenly backward as if someone had pushed him. The look on his face was one of comical confusion and then recollection. He turned abruptly and strode away without explanation – not to the construction site but to the other end of the table where Anna was looking after the desserts. Rosie stared after him, stunned, not only at his words but also at his sudden unexplained departure. He rounded the dessert table and ushered his mother to the side of the yard. Rosie continued watching as they entered into an intense discussion.

Ruthie interrupted her observations. "I'm going home to lay my *boppli* down. Do you want me to give you a lift so you can put Seth down for his nap?"

"*Ach*, would you?" Rosie tore her gaze away from Hezekiah and Anna, deep in conversation. "That would be an answer to prayer. *Danke*."

The two sisters prepared to leave the construction site with legitimate excuses for laying their little ones down.

Minutes later, Rosie settled Seth in the buggy, then glanced toward the construction site. The glare of the sun outlined a tall, impressive figure. She squinted and lifted a hand to shade her eyes, blocking the sun's direct rays. It was Hezekiah. He gave her a slow, thoughtful nod, his deep-set eyes staring steadily back into hers.

'Why do I feel he has something to say to me?' Rosie shook her head, trying to shake the thought. But the image of him standing against the unfinished barn stayed with her. Thankfully, Ruthie's words broke through her meanderings. "Are you ready to go, Rosie?"

"*Ja*," she looked over at her sister, attempting to put all thoughts of Hezekiah out of her mind. But her mind was very singular and insisted on having its own way: 'He isn't anything like Dennis. He's not a mean person; at least when he was a boy at school, he hadn't been. Now, was he a tease? That was a different story!'

At school, the teacher had assigned the seat behind her to Hezekiah. Rosie recalled all the times he had tied her braids together. When she demanded he leave her alone, he teased further. "Ya ain't mad at me, are ya, Rosie? Not my sweet Rosie." One day he had brought a rose to school for her, and he'd endured the ribbing of the other boys; the memory was as clear as if it had happened the day before. He had murmured to her, "It don't matter, 'cause I'd do anythin' fer, my sweet Rosie," then winked at her.

Rosie closed her eyes and swallowed, remembering the day almost four years before – the day that had changed the course of her life forever. 'My friends wanted to go to Canada's Wonderland, but *Dat* wouldn't let me go.' She recalled confiding in her friends that she was going to leave home. Hezekiah and the others had tried to reason with her. "Don't go, Rosie. Stay and work it out. There will be other times." But she hadn't listened. Upset and strong-willed, she decided to do something about it. Before the week was out, she had bought a bus ticket and headed toward Toronto.

Ruthie broke into her daydream world. "There was a *gut* turnout today, ain't?"

Rosie glanced over at her sister and nodded. "*Ja*, the barn will be up in no time. I'm glad you could take us home. Seth gets real tired once he's eaten."

"Me too," Ruthie laughed.

Rosie adjusted her hold on Seth and fell back into her thoughts. Getting on a bus had been one thing, but looking for a job hadn't been easy. The only one available was serving in a pub. That's where she met Dennis and some of his biker friends. At first, it felt good having Dennis organize her life, telling her where to go and how and when to work. It made her think he cared, that he only had her best interests at heart. 'Wrong! Boy, had she been wrong! He was a control freak.'

Eventually, one thing had led to another, and she became pregnant. She remembered thinking that Dennis would change once he discovered she was having his baby. Instead, he became mean and beat her; sometimes, he wouldn't look for an excuse. Before long, she was expecting again. When she could no longer hide her bulging stomach, Dennis took his rage out on her, breaking her arm. Scared out of her wits, Rosie contacted her dad. The night her dad came and took Seth away, Dennis beat her, worse than any other time. The other beatings had been a walk in the park compared to that last one. She was lucky to get out with her life. 'Now, here I am,' she concluded, relieved. 'I'll never give any *mann* that power over me ever again,' she vowed while hugging her sleeping baby close.

Thanking Ruthie for the ride home, Rosie carried her sleeping boy into the house where all the Yoder girls had grown up. Climbing the stairs, she lay him in his cot, watching him slumber in the sweet innocence of the young. Rosie sat in the rocker in their room and picked up her needlework. There were only five more appliques to sew, and then she could take the finished pieces back to Esther. After sewing another applique, she lay down on the bed to rest her eyes. What seemed like minutes ended with Seth's repetitive voice, "Mama. Mama." She tried to brush it aside; then, her eyes flew open, startled. 'Why would Hezekiah be in my bedroom?' But Seth giggled as he stood up in his crib, jumping up and down while holding onto the bars. "Mama." He repeated until Rosie sat on the side of her bed. The grandfather clock downstairs chimed four o'clock. 'I guess I was more tired than I thought,' she rubbed the back of her neck and went over to the crib to pick her son up.

~.~.~.~

Wednesday morning, Rosie and Seth headed to her weekly housekeeping job. The wind had risen again, breaking the warm spell they had enjoyed for eleven days. Rosie sighed her resignation, 'Winter's on its way.' She was thankful that the closed-in family buggy kept some of the wind off her and Seth.

"Make sure ya cover the horse over with this blanket," Tobiah threw a thick rug into the buggy. "An' don't leave it too late *kummin'* back. It's gettin' dark earlier, an' with the weather turnin', it'll get darker earlier than usual."

Rose assured him she'd be home in good time and set off out the drive at a fast trot. Within twenty minutes, they pulled into the farm. As promised, she covered the horse and tied him to a tree, away from the worst of the wind.

"*Kumme* Seth," she held him tight, shielding him from the wind the best she could. Within a couple of minutes, they were inside. Rosie started the kindling already set in the stove's firebox, and before long, the kitchen began warming up. She worked quickly, not wanting her parents to worry. The housekeeping money was in its usual place, in the bread box on the counter. She stuffed the money into the bag alongside Seth's snack. Rosie worked methodically through the house. First, the kitchen, then through the lower rooms of the house, and on to the second floor. Frequently, she glanced out the window. Already the sky had darkened. With Seth bundled and the stove shut down, she made her way to the horse three hours later. She placed Seth inside the protection of the buggy and walked forward to pull the heavy rug from the horse. There was a hay net tied in front of the animal. Rosie looked at it baffled, then looked around. 'The *alt* farmer must have tied it there.' She would have liked to thank him, but where would she even begin to look? Deciding it could wait, Rosie shoved the blanket inside the buggy beside Seth, then climbed up to the seat. Forty-five minutes later, Tobiah met her at the barn, led the horse inside, and returned to carry Seth to the house.

"Ya only got back in time," Tobiah looked to the skies. "We got snow *kummin'*."

Rosie followed close behind, holding her cape closed at the neck.

Miriam met them at the door and picked Seth from Tobiah's arms.

"I'm goin' ta the Mill an' let the men go early. I'll be back as soon as I can. I want ta run a line from the barn ta the *haus* in case this storm sets in." Then he was gone, fighting strong gusts of wind that blew from one angle and then from another, seemingly having difficulty deciding which direction it should blow.

Rosie warmed chilled fingers over the stove, unhooked her cape, and hung it on a peg. "Have we got enough wood for the *nacht*?" She looked at her mom.

"*Ja*. Your *daed* chopped wood this morning and piled it in the woodshed. We should have plenty."

Rosie nodded, relieved. "It's not very nice out there; it took me twice as long to *kumme* home as when I went out this morning."

"You might want to rethink going out on days like this," Miriam looked at her with a worried frown.

"*Ja*. On Meeting Sunday, I'll say something to Anna, so she can tell the *mann* that owns the farm. I never see him, or I'd tell him myself."

"Well, where is he?" Miriam asked, puzzled.

"I'm not sure. In the barn, I guess. Although Anna said he generally goes to Kitchener's sale barns on Wednesdays, I know he didn't go today."

Miriam looked at her, mystified.

"He tied a hay net out for the horse," Rosie explained.

"That was thoughtful," Miriam dropped another hardwood log into the stove.

"*Ja.* I thought so, too." The two women hurried to put the soup on the stove.

"*Gut* soup weather," Rosie commented and placed the soup bowls in the warming closet over the stove. She looked to see what Seth was doing; he was content, stacking the wooden blocks his grandfather had made for him. Turning to the pantry, Rosie gathered the soup spoons and placed them on the table before cutting bread for sandwiches. It was none too soon; boots stomping on the side porch told her, '*Dat's kumming* in for lunch.'

~ ~ ~

If anyone causes one of these little ones to stumble,
It would be better for them to have a millstone hung
Around their neck and drowned in the depths of the sea
~ Matthew 18:6 ~

Chapter 8
Healing Wounds

Six inches of fluffy snow blanketed the ground, greeting everyone the following morning. The snow had drifted higher at the side of the house and around stands of trees.

"It won't stay, it's only October, but it's early this year. We haven't even had Thanksgivin' yet, an' here we have our first snowfall." Tobiah warmed his chilled hands over the woodstove as Miriam and Rosie put breakfast on the table.

"I'd like to take Seth outside after breakfast and make a *snowmann*. Maybe I could show him how to make a snow *engel*!" Rosie commented, smiling at her parents.

Miriam and Tobiah stopped what they were doing, and looked at their daughter, then at one another. Rosie's excitement was contagious and filled their hearts with joy.

"Make sure ya bundle up *gut*. It's cold out there," Tobiah recommended, a slow grin covering his face.

"I'll hunt up a spare scarf to wrap around the *snowmann's* neck," Miriam offered. "It's *gut* to have *kinder* again; I've missed seeing a *snowmann* in the yard." She smiled from Rosie to Tobiah, pleased, then began dishing out their hot multi-grain cereal.

Following breakfast, Rosie upended the bag she had taken to her house cleaning job, looking for Seth's mitts.

The money she had crammed into the bag tumbled out along with the little mittens.

"*Ach*, we've been so busy the last few days, I near forgot I put this in here," she remarked aloud.

"What's that, Rosie?" Miriam looked up, stopping in mid-stride, kneading the dough.

"The money the *mann* leaves for me every week for cleaning the *haus*." She looked at the solid manly handwriting on the piece of paper. '*Danke* for doing a *gut* job. Leave a list when you need more supplies, and I'll pick them up.' Rosie turned the piece of paper over. It wasn't signed. She shrugged and looked at the bills, becoming visibly shocked.

"What is it?" Miriam asked, preparing to divide the bread dough into loaf pans.

Rosie read the note aloud. "But that's not all, *Mamm*; there's twice as much money as I usually get."

"Well, the note did say you're doing a *gut* job; he must be grateful, is all," Miriam assured her, resuming her chore at hand.

"Still, it's a surprise."

"It's a nice surprise." Miriam smiled endearingly at her. "Heaven knows you're long since overdue. Next time we're making pies, you could take one over and leave it as a token of appreciation."

"*Ja*. That's a *gut* idea, *Mamm*," Rosie's eyes gleamed in response to her mother's suggestion. "That's a real *gut* idea."

The following Sunday was Meeting Sunday. Rosie was anxious to find Anna and talk with her. Following the final prayer, she craned her neck, searching for the woman who had become so important to her.

"Anna, how are you?" Rosie smiled broadly, shifting Seth to her other hip.

"I'm doing real *gut*. It's busier than I'd like it to be, but it goes along with my job," Anna laughed. "How are you? Your cheeks are getting some color in them."

"I'm feeling a lot stronger. I wanted to say *danke* for finding me that *hauskeeping* job."

"Well, I know of more if you're interested," Anna returned. "While I have you here, I wanted to say how pleased the *mann* is with how you are looking after his *haus*. But he does have one concern."

Rosie's eyebrows puckered together. She didn't like the word 'but.' To her, it was always conditional and negated the words before. Giving her full attention to what Anna had to say, Rosie waited with an element of trepidation.

"Last Wednesday, he was concerned about you driving in such bad weather."

Rosie expelled a sigh of relief and nodded in understanding. "*Ja. Mamm* and *Daed* were too. They think anytime the weather is snowy or windy like last week, I shouldn't take chances on the road."

"I'm glad you agree. Otherwise, how do you like it there?"

"It's exactly the job I need. He doesn't mind that I'm taking Seth, does he?"

"He didn't say a word about that. The only thing he's concerned about is you driving in bad weather."

"*Danke*, Anna. I guess we all agree then." Rosie nodded appreciatively, then added, "He put extra money in the bread box last week, so *Mamm* and I thought we'll bake an extra one since we're baking pies. You wouldn't happen to know what pie he's partial to, would you?"

Anna chuckled. "Without a doubt, Bumbleberry. But it's a little late in the season to be making Bumbleberry pie."

"*Ja*," Rosie became thoughtful. "I know *Mamm,* and I can put our heads together and *kumme* up with something," she smiled at Anna appreciatively. "Are you headed toward the kitchen? I'll walk over with you."

"*Ja*. Before we get there, I have a confession …" Anna began, but before she could finish, Seth started to call, "Mama. Mama."

Rosie followed his intent gaze. She smiled, her face brightening. 'Where Hezekiah is concerned, Seth is like a magnet. After Dennis' abuse, I would have thought he'd be scared to death of men. But *daed* and Hezekiah are two of his most favorite people.' Rosie laughed and looked at Anna. "Seth does like your *sohn*."

"I have to agree with him," Anna leaned toward Rosie. "I'm kind of partial to him myself." They laughed companionably.

Hezekiah approached, chuckling. "There's no escapin' yer boy," he smiled at Rosie. "It's like he knows where I am before I do." He took Seth from Rosie's arms.

"If you're busy, don't feel you need to take him," Rosie hurriedly assured him.

Becoming quiet, Hezekiah returned soberly. "Rosie, I'm not busy. Even if I was, I'd always make time fer my Buddy." He smiled at Seth, lifting him high and setting the little boy on his shoulders. Seth giggled and held tight to

Hezekiah's head, knocking Hezekiah's felt hat, so it sat askew on his head.

They walked toward the house. "*Danke*," Rosie gave a tight smile in Hezekiah's direction, wondering at his sudden seriousness. "I know he starts getting heavy after a while."

"No problem. We men need ta stick tagether, don't we, Buddy?" Hezekiah shifted Seth on his shoulders and straightened his hat.

Arriving at the house, Rosie and Anna entered the kitchen while Hezekiah and Seth searched for Charles Woerner.

Charles, seeing his son, stood up to get Hezekiah's attention. He chuckled to himself. 'It looks ta me like my *sohn* is makin' a statement by carryin' Rosie's boy about all the time.'

As was the custom of The People, the church leaders first went through the line-up for food. Then the older men of the district, followed by the single men, and finally, the younger boys. Theirs' is a strict hierarchy, instilling respect for the older men, and the young boys didn't dare push their way out of turn.

An hour later, Hezekiah searched for Rosie; Seth had eaten and was sleeping in his arms.
It would be the last time the food would be set outside on the tables. The weather had turned quickly, as only the weather can in that part of Ontario, cradled by two of the Great Lakes.

When Hezekiah found Rosie shivering at one of the tables laden with food, he offered. "I'll give ya a ride home, Rosie. That way ya can lay yer *boppli* down."

Rosie looked at him, surprised. "*Ja*. It has turned chilly out. Ain't so?' Her teeth chattered. "I should have worn my cape," she commented. "Let me tell *Mamm*, and I'll be ready to go." Turning, Rosie looked to see if she could locate her mother.

Anna overheard their conversation as she came down the steps from the kitchen. "Rosie, let me tell her. You shouldn't be out in this cold dampness; you're still getting back on your feet. Go with Hezekiah, and I'll let her know you've gone on home," she encouraged.

"*Ach, danke* Anna. This dampness has me chilled right to the bone. Tell *Mamm* I'll get the fire going, so it will be warm in the *haus* when they get back."

"I'll let her know. You go on with Hezekiah." She asked her son, "Have you got a blanket in the buggy to wrap Rosie and Seth in?"

"*Ja*. I'll get them bundled up, *Mamm*," he assured and ushered Rosie to his buggy, Seth sleeping snuggly in the crook of his neck.

While Hezekiah quickly put his horse into the buggy, Rosie held her sleeping son. She watched as Hezekiah lay a thick lap robe over the seat and surrendered Seth to him when he reached for the sleeping boy. After ensuring she safely climbed up to the buggy seat, he settled Seth back into her arms. Then, he carefully covered them with the remaining blanket and climbed up to sit beside her.

His gentleness and concern touched Rosie, and tears collected in her eyes.

"What's wrong, Rosie?" He looked at her closely, eyebrows knitted together in a frown.

She shook her head and bit her lower lip to stay her emotions. "It's just, that you're so kind to us," she gulped, unable to finish.

"And I always will be." He held her eyes, checked the lap robe around her shoulders, and then chirped to the horse to move forward.

A half-hour later, Hezekiah turned into the Yoder drive. He hurried Rosie and Seth inside. While Rosie stood in the center of the cold kitchen, Hezekiah lit the wood in the stove. Once the fire was going, he turned the damper back on the stovepipe. Gently, he took Seth from Rosie's arms. "You'll need ta show me where his room is. I don't know the layout of yer *haus.*"

Rosie hurried ahead of him. Once Seth was in his crib, she removed his jacket and shoes and covered him with a blanket. Hezekiah stayed with her, watched, and followed her back down the steps. "Will you stay for something hot to drink before you leave?" Rosie invited.

"*Danke, nee.* I want ta get my horse home an' give him a hot mash ta help him warm up. Will ya be alright?"

"*Ja. Danke* for bringing us home."

"It was my pleasure," he placed his black felt hat over his sandy curls, then he was gone.

Rosie stood at the window and watched him drape the lap robe across his knees. Immediately, she felt guilty. He had generously wrapped them in his only protection against the cold, and she hadn't even had the foresight to share it with him. Rosie lifted her hand in farewell as he headed out the drive. He nodded in response as he clucked to his horse, and then they were gone. For some unknown reason, Rosie felt an emptiness deep down in her stomach, suddenly feeling alone. Then it dawned on her. 'I have no idea where he lives.' She should have asked him; she supposed he probably lived with his parents. With that uppermost on her mind, she turned back into the kitchen to tend the fire.

~ ~ ~

For I will restore you to health.
And I will heal your wounds,
Declares the LORD
~ Jeremiah 30:17 ~

Chapter 9

Lean Not in Your Own Understanding

"Red in the morning, shepherds take warning," Miriam quipped, looking out the window as the sun rose over the snow-skiffed fields - the sky seemingly shimmered an orangey red.

"*Ja*. We'll have a white Thanksgivin', fer sure." Tobiah finished washing at the sink and sat down at the table. He glanced over at Rosie. "I put a hay net full of hay inta the back of the buggy; it'll give the horse something ta do an' keep him warm while yer cleanin' *haus*."

"*Danke, Dat.*"

"Are ya sure ya don't want me ta drive ya over?"

Rosie looked at her dad, surprised. "*Nee*. I should be alright, *Dat*," she carried the hot breakfast to the table.

"Keep Seth covered, or he'll get frostbite."

'There it is again, the control,' Rosie's mind registered. Feeling the age-old rebellion rising within her, she glanced at her dad and saw the concern written on his face. '*Nee!*' She corrected herself. 'It's not control! It's out of concern because *daed* genuinely cares for Seth's and my well-being.' Had she misread her dad's restrictions years ago? Had it been because he had cared about her, and she had taken it as trying to control her activities? Tears threatened. To hide her emotions, she turned quickly to pull the coffee mugs from the warming closet above the stove.

"Don't worry. It only takes us twenty minutes to get there, *Dat*, and I'll bundle him up warm."

"You too," he added.

Rosie smiled to herself. "It's so *gut* to be home with you and *Mamm*. You have no idea how much I missed you."

"Us too, Rosie girl. Us too." He nodded, a softness touching his weathered face.

After silent prayer, they sat at the table and dug into the hardy breakfast. For the Amish farming community, breakfast is the day's most important meal.

Following breakfast, Rosie helped straighten the kitchen. Bundled against the cold, Tobiah headed to the barn to harness the horse. By eight, Rosie and Seth, wrapped in a thick lap robe, were ready to make the drive to her housekeeping job. The boxed Bumbleberry pie was safe, tucked under the seat. "I should be back by lunchtime," she smiled at her dad and turned to wave to her mother.

"We'll be waitin' fer ya. When ya get there, cover the horse over. Ya don't want his muscles tyin' up after drivin' him when it's so cold, or he'll be too lame ta make the trip back."

"I'll trot him slow, *Dat,* so he won't get overheated." Mentally she realized that the trip would take a little bit longer. She clucked to the animal, and they headed out the drive.

Rosie turned into her employer's drive a half hour later. The longer drive made her thankful for the scarf and mitts she had put on before leaving home. While tying the horse to a tree, a familiar voice greeted, "*Guten morgen*, Rosie."

Rosie turned abruptly; at the same time, Seth uttered a pleased, "Mama."

"Hezekiah!" she smiled broadly and a little breathlessly, surprising herself with how pleased she was to see him.

"*Kumme*," he picked Seth up. "I'll walk ya to the *haus*."

"I didn't know you'd be here," Rosie walked beside him. "Are you visiting?" For some reason, that reminded her of the pie. "*Ach*, wait here, and I'll be right back. I forgot something." She hurried back to the buggy, not waiting for Hezekiah's response. "And I promised *Dat* I'd cover the horse as soon as I got here," she threw over her shoulder.

"Leave it. I'll do it as soon as ya get in the *haus*," Hezekiah assured, following her.

Rosie carefully extracted the box containing the pie from under the seat.

"What ya got there?" Hezekiah raised his head, doing his best to see inside the box.

"A pie for the *mann* that owns the *haus*."

"Now, ya have me really interested," Hezekiah grinned broadly.

"It's not for you," Rosie looked at him pointedly and laughed at the disappointment on his face. By this time, they had reached the house.

"Let me settle yer horse, an' I'll be right back in." Hezekiah set Seth on the floor.

"Bring the *alt mann* that owns the farm with you," Rosie instructed as she removed their mitts and winter clothing.

Hezekiah looked at her, raising an eyebrow at her request.

Ten minutes later, stomping on the porch announced the arrival of the men.

'Finally, I get to meet this elusive *mann*,' she smiled nervously. 'At least Hezekiah's here,' she pondered, thankful for his presence.

Hezekiah walked into the warm kitchen and removed his hat and coat, hooking them over a peg beside the door. Rosie looked around him expectantly. "Didn't the *alt* farmer *kumme* to the *haus* with you?" Her eyebrows drew together, disappointed.

"Rosie. There's something we need ta talk about." He pulled out a chair at the kitchen table and sat down, and immediately Seth climbed onto his lap. "When my *Mamm* asked ya ta look after this *haus*, can ya tell me what she said?"

"*Ja*. Sure." Rosie nodded. "She told me she was cleaning a *haus* for an *alt* bachelor. But she was getting too busy with new *Mamm's* and their *bopplies* being born. She said she couldn't look after it, so she asked me if I wanted to."

"*Alt* bachelor, huh?" Hezekiah snorted.

"*Ja*. She said he was set in his ways and wouldn't give me any trouble because most Wednesdays, he was at the Kitchener sales."

"My *Mamm* said that?" His eyebrows raised.

"*Ja,*" Rosie dragged the word out and looked skeptically at Hezekiah. "Is there something wrong, Hezekiah?"

"*Nee*. There's nothing wrong….," he emphasized the word, wrong. "Set in his ways, is he? An *alt* bachelor, is he?"

"*Ja*. That's what she said." Rosie nodded slowly, suddenly wary, and looked at Hezekiah closely.

"Funny. I never thought of myself as bein' *alt* or set in my ways." Hezekiah chuckled and shook his head, a funny look on his face. "*Alt!*" He muttered with an element of disgust.

"You!? You're the *alt mann*!?" Rosie gawked at him.

"Yup. It seems my *Mamm* was workin' both sides of the fence. And when I found out, I knew it wasn't right not tellin' ya an' puttin' ya straight."

"*Ach*," Rosie let out a long moan and slowly sank onto one of the other chairs. "I guess this means you don't want me cleaning for you, doesn't it?"

"*Nee*. On the contrary. I think yer doin' a *wunderbar gut* job.

"I don't think she meant any harm," Rosie defended Anna.

"Perhaps not." Hezekiah raised his eyebrows in a quirk and smiled mischievously at Rosie. "Ya want ta get in on a little fun?"

"What kind of fun?" Rosie looked at him, afraid to commit to his idea of fun.

He crossed his arms over his chest. "I don't know yet, but you'll be the first ta know when I do." He rose from the chair. "So, I guess that pie's fer me, right?" He walked over to look in the box.

"Well, if you're the *alt,* set in his ways, bachelor, your *Mamm* was talking about, I guess it is," Rosie teased. Then it dawned on her, and she looked at him, surprised. "*Ach,* she knew that too!" At his raised eyebrows of inquiry, Rosie enlarged. "That your favorite pie is Bumbleberry."

"Really? Ya made me Bumbleberry pie, Rosie? I can taste it already."

"Do you want me to warm a piece up with *kaffee* before you go back outside?"

"A piece?" He looked crestfallen. "Just one piece, Rosie? Ya sure do know how ta torture a *mann.*"

Rosie laughed at his woeful expression. "Well, I can warm another piece up for you if you like it."

"Ya won't ever hear me sayin' *nee* ta that." He rubbed his hands together in anticipation.

Rosie laughed and busied herself about the kitchen.

"I know a *gut* joke ta play on my *Mamm.* I'm not goin' ta let her know you, and I have had our little chat. While yer with us, I'm goin' ta ask her ta introduce me to my new *hauskeeper.* Then watch her try ta squirm outa that one." Hezekiah chuckled mischievously.

Rosie laughed at the gleam in his eye. It was apparent Hezekiah and his mom had a history of playing practical jokes on each other. An involuntary giggle escaped her; she could only imagine the outcome. On deeper reflection, she knew she couldn't begin to imagine the result, and she laughed.

Hezekiah, as he predicted, ended up having two pieces of pie. "Rosie, this pie is some *gut,*" he made appreciative sounds with each mouthful. "Ya wouldn't like ta *kumme* here ta live an' bake pies fer me all the time, would ya?"

Rosie smiled. This was the Hezekiah with which she was familiar, the joker. "I don't need to *kumme* here to live to make pies," she laughed. "Besides, you'll get lazy and start looking like a pie if I did."

"I promise I won't," he held up a hand as if taking an oath.

"You need to go back outside, so I can get your *haus* cleaned. I promised *Mamm* and *Dat* I'd be home for lunch."

"Will it help if'n I take Seth outside with me?"

"*Ja.* That way, I can whip through without worrying about where he is. You'll keep a close eye on him, won't you?"

"I won't take my eyes off him," he promised with an element of seriousness, then added light-heartedly, "Don't take the rest of that pie with ya. I want ta have more before I go ta bed *tanacht.*"

"*Danke* for taking Seth outside, and *nee,* I won't take the pie," she assured and busied herself dressing Seth before tidying the kitchen.

Two hours later, stomping on the back porch told Rosie her men were coming inside. She stopped. 'My men? Where did that *kumme* from?' The porch door swung open, putting a stop to her thoughts. She knelt and gave Seth a big hug; he smelled of hay and straw and the fresh outdoors. Holding him at arm's length, she smiled at his rosy cheeks, then up at Hezekiah. "*Danke,* this is the healthiest I've ever seen him."

"Then you'll have ta *kumme* more often. He's a *gut* little worker. We stacked wood in the shed before *kummin'* in, didn't we, Buddy?" He tousled Seth's hair. "I'll take him back outside with me so he won't get too hot. If'n yer near ready ta leave, I'll get yer horse ready."

"*Ja.* I'll get my things and be right out." Rosie closed the door behind them, hurried to collect everything, and put on her cape and bonnet. Minutes later, she and Seth were bundled in the buggy, ready to leave. "Next time I *kumme,* I'll make you chicken and dumplings, if you like?" She swallowed nervously; it had dawned on her that Hezekiah might read more into her cooking a meal for him than she intended. Her concerns were swept away when Hezekiah's face lit up in anticipation.

"Really, Rosie? Ya'd do that fer me? Ya know how ta make a *mann* feel like he's in heaven." He chuckled, "The offer still stands. Ya can move in any time ya want."

Rosie laughed. "Hezekiah, you always were the biggest tease."

"Who said I was teasing, Rosie?" He looked into her dark blue eyes, and a lopsided grin played slowly at his mouth. "But not before we're married, eh?" He chuckled, and his eyebrows quirked at her look of shock. "I'll see ya next week unless ya want ta *kumme* sooner." He slapped the horse on the rump and raised his hand in salute as the buggy moved past him.

Fortunately, the horse knew his way home because Rosie was too flustered to direct him back to their barn. 'I'll just stop cleaning *haus* for him,' she decided. But, the thought of Seth's unhappiness squelched that idea. She looked at his rosy red cheeks. 'You can't take that away from him, Rosie,' she admonished herself. 'This is the first time he's been so happy.' With a sigh of resignation, Rosie continued brainstorming. 'Maybe, I should tell him the way it is. That I'll never allow another *mann* to have control over me ever again.'

Tightening the lines, Rosie made contact with the horse's mouth. It was as if taking control of driving the horse gave her license to take control of her life. Happy with her decision, she drove the animal home.

Tobiah met her at the barn. "Is everything going alright, Rosie?" He took hold of the horse's bridle.

Rosie looked at her dad suspiciously. When he didn't enlarge but lifted Seth out of the buggy, she figured she was being overly sensitive. Wisely, she decided to drop the matter. "*Ja*. Each time I go there, it seems to get easier - I expect it's because I'm getting used to where everything is now."

Her dad mumbled something in response and handed Seth to her. "I'll settle the horse and be up fer lunch in ten minutes. Let yer *Mamm* know, would ya?" He led the horse forward to the buggy shed. Quickly, his experienced fingers unwrapped the straps holding the animal between the shafts, then led him to the barn.

"How was your morning, Rosie?" Miriam asked as she bustled about the kitchen.

"*Gut, danke Mamm*," Rosie removed Seth's jacket and mitts before shrugging out of her own. "*Dat* said he'd be up in ten minutes or so."

"I figured he'd be in now that you're home," Miriam smiled in her direction.

Rosie hung her cape on a peg beside the door. Glancing over her shoulder, "*Mamm,* do you think it's right to clean in a single *mann's haus*?"

Miriam stopped what she was doing and looked at her daughter, baffled. "Rosie, you knew before you went that the *haus* belonged to an *alt* bachelor. What's changed your mind?"

"The fact that the bachelor isn't all that *alt,* and it's someone we know."

Rosie and Miriam's talk was interrupted by Tobiah stomping his boots as he entered the side porch. "Is it something you'd feel comfortable talking about around your *Daed*? He's very knowledgeable, and he'd see it from a *mann's* perspective," Miriam looked kindly at her daughter.

"*Ja.* It wouldn't bother me to talk to *Dat* about it," Rosie agreed.

"*Gut.* Then let's leave it until after lunch." Miriam began ladling thick homemade vegetable soup into bowls. Rosie, content to leave her worries for the moment, carried the soup bowls to the table.

Lunch finished, Tobiah sat back in his chair and sipped at his coffee. Miriam didn't leave the table, as she usually did following a meal, and opened the subject. "Rosie wondered if we would share our opinion about her cleaning this *alt* bachelor's *haus*." She nodded toward Rosie, encouraging her daughter to share her concerns.

"Ahh," Tobiah nodded. "Are ya havin' a change of heart, Rosie girl?"

"Not really, *Dat*. It's just Anna told me the *haus* belonged to an *alt*, confirmed bachelor. Well," she shrugged. "I went into the job with the idea that the *mann* was, well, *alt.* "

"Is he botherin' ya?"

"*Nee.*"

"An' he's still payin' ya."

"*Ja, Dat.* Last week more than he should have."

"So, what's changed?"

"Well, today I met the owner."

"Ahh," Tobiah nodded knowingly. "And?"

"Well, he isn't all that *alt.* "

"An' probably not a confirmed bachelor either, I'm guessin'." Tobiah looked at his daughter and chuckled.

"*Ja.* Furthermore, it's someone we all know. I don't know if it's proper for me to continue cleaning *haus*, is all." Rosie's voice petered off, and she fidgeted with the handle on her cup.

"Rosie, Hezekiah will never hurt ya."

"How did you know it was Hezekiah?" Rosie asked, surprised.

"Cause the day of the barn raisin', he came an' talked ta me. He'd just found out it was you doin' the cleanin', an' he'd never go against my wishes. So, I told him what I thought. That he is an honorable young *mann*, an' if'n it was something ya wanted ta do, I'd not stand in yer way. I also told him he needed ta sit down an' have a talk with ya. Secrets like that ain't *gut.*"

"You did, *Dat*?"

"*Ja*, I did. So, if'n nothing's changed, I guess I'd say it's a nice way ta make a little money. Seth sure has taken a likin' ta him."

Following her dad's admission, Rosie shared more with her parents. "Hezekiah took Seth outside, giving me a chance to get the *haus* cleaned. I told him I'd make chicken and dumplings the next time I went. You don't suppose that was too forward, do you?" She looked from her mom to her dad.

Tobiah chuckled. "He'll be wantin' ya ta stay there, next thing we know. Didn't ya take him a pie, taday?"

Rosie blushed. Her dad was closer to the truth than she cared to admit. "*Ja*, but that was before I knew who owned the *haus*."

"As far as I'm concerned, ya won't find any better *mann* than Hezekiah Woerner. He's a hard worker, honorable an' *kummes* from a *gut* family. Anything else ya was wantin' ta talk about?"

"*Nee*." Rosie sat in shock, taken aback by her dad's approval of Hezekiah. Tobiah pushed the chair back from the table and stood up slowly.

"That was a *gut* lunch," he directed to Miriam. "Warmed me up inside real *gut*. He pulled on his coat, grabbed his hat from the peg beside the door, and went out to pull his boots on.

"Do you feel better having talked to your *daed*?" Miriam smiled warmly at her middle daughter.

"*Ja Mamm. Danke.* Sometimes things don't seem so big when there is someone to talk to."

"*Ja.* Sometimes those obstacles in our heads are bigger than reality. Eighty-five percent of the things we worry about never come about."

Rosie nodded. "It's *gut* to have you and *Dat* to talk to."

"I'm glad we're here for one another," Miriam smiled and nodded toward her grandson, his head bobbing sleepily. "You need to carry Seth upstairs - his outing with Hezekiah has him all worn out."

~ ~ ~

Trust in the LORD with all your heart
And lean not on your own understanding
~ Proverbs 3:5 ~

Chapter 10
Kindness and Compassion

Every second Monday in October, countless Thanksgiving turkeys grace the threshold of many Canadian ovens, both Amish and English alike. It is a time when family members get together, prepare for the bountiful results of the fall harvest in myriad ways, and enjoy one another's company before the winter winds and snow settle in.

For the first time in years, the Woerner homestead was full of family members, bringing a sense of contentment to the hearts of Anna and Charles. Everyone found their place at the long harvest table, chatting and joking with one another while inhaling the tempting aromas of the feast. Many bowls were heaped with honeyed carrots, pepper squash, mashed potatoes, and turkey dressing.

Charles Jr. placed a sizeable oval platter before his dad, presenting him with the enormous golden bird. Everyone became silent; all eyes followed its path from the stove to the table and, taking Charles Sr.'s example, bowed heads for the prayer of thanksgiving. Today, being a special day, he prayed aloud a Thanksgiving grace and concluded, "We *danke* Heavenly *Vater* fer family gathered 'round this table. An' we ask fer a blessin' upon those unable ta be here. Keep Leah an' Hiram, wherever they are. Amen." The others at the table nodded, adding their own silent prayers for their missing family.

Anna smiled appreciatively at her husband and touched him fleetingly on the shoulder as she hurried to the stove to pull rolls out of the oven. While Charles carved the turkey, everyone began passing their plates, some requesting white meat, others dark, and Hezekiah asking for a drumstick. Murmurs of appreciation followed as everyone began to eat. Anna, Helena, and Naomi had outdone themselves in making the feast that lay before them. Emptied serving dishes were moved to the sideboard and replaced with coffee and slices of pumpkin pie. The greatest compliment to the cooks was seeing the food disappear until everyone surpassed overflowing.

Naomi, Eli, and Perry were bundled up by three, ready to make the trip home so Eli could get the milking done. Hezekiah also headed out to feed his calves, promising to return and eat a light supper with his parents. After the calves were fed and settled for the night, he returned to help his dad and brother with the evening milking, then joined his parents in the *Dawdi haus* afterward. Once supper was over, Hezekiah sat chatting about farming with his dad while Anna straightened the kitchen.

"Yer next bunch of calves should be ready ta go ta *markt* soon," Charles commented.

"*Ja.* Another two weeks."

"Have ya got the truck ordered?"

"*Ja.* It'll arrive at the usual time – *gut* an' early. Are ya *kummin'*?"

"Fer certain. I'll get in touch with our driver later this week."

"That'd be *gut*," Hezekiah nodded deep in thought.

"I imagine a lot of turkeys got ate taday," the elder Woerner commented with a chuckle.

"*Ja*," Hezekiah nodded, agreeing, his attentiveness to the conversation at hand drifting.

"An' fer the rest of the week, too," Charles glanced over at Hezekiah, puzzled at his son's sudden withdrawal.

"*Ja. Ja.*" Hezekiah nodded, agreeing in a distracted way.

"I suppose it'll be sweltering hot tamorrow, too," the elder Woerner remarked, a knowing smirk on his face.

Anna looked at her husband and frowned, wondering what had gotten into him.

"*Ja... Ja...*" Hezekiah nodded again, his thoughts now a hundred miles away, remembering the Bumbleberry pie Rosie had made for him and the promise of chicken and dumplings to come.

"Odd thing, that boy callin' ya *Mamma*," his dad tried another tactic.

"How's that, *Dat*?" Hezekiah blinked, confused about what his dad was saying.

"I said. How do ya figure Rosie's *kinder* callin' ya *Mamma*?"

"*Ja*. He's a neat little guy. But I sure ain't figured out why he calls me *Mamma*." Hezekiah chuckled.

"Probably 'cause his *Mamm* is the only thing he can associate with what's *gut*. So, anyone else nice ta him is automatically called *Mamma*," Charles presumed.

"Could be," Hezekiah shrugged, coming out of his daydream world.

"Have you ever heard him say anything else?" Anna got in on the conversation.

Hezekiah looked at his mother, stumped. "*Kumme* ta mention it, I don't think I have. He's usually pretty quiet. Ya'd never know he was in the room," Hezekiah studied his mom, wondering what she was getting at.

"He doesn't make noises when he's playing, like Charles' two little ones?" Anna asked. "I wonder if he has a hearing problem," she pondered.

Next time Rosie's over, I'll check with her." Hezekiah became thoughtful. "Then again, it could be he just ain't talkin' yet – he's only about two – ain't he?" Hezekiah stood up, putting an end to their talk about Seth. "I better get home. The calves won't understand me sleepin' in tamorrow mornin'," he shrugged into his coat.

"I'll *kumme* out with ya, an' hold the lantern while ya harness yer horse."

"*Danke, Dat. Danke* fer a *gut* Thanksgivin' *Mamm*," Hezekiah opened the door, thinking, 'I'm glad my place is only one line over.' He sighed, wishing he didn't have to go out in the cold and snow.

~.~.~.~

Rosie and Seth made their way to Hezekiah's farm the Wednesday following Thanksgiving. He met them and took the horse to the stable. Minutes later, he returned to the house, carrying a plucked chicken. He held it up like he was presenting a golden goose. "Ya did say I could look forward ta chicken an' dumplin's," a goofy grin covered his face.

Rosie laughed at his antics. "You better let me have that bird, so I can start cooking it. The best chicken and dumplings is when the meat is cooked so well it's falling off the bone."

Hezekiah took a deep breath as if breathing in and imagining the pleasing aroma of the finished meal. "How long before it's ready ta eat?"

"It'll be ready for you to eat by lunchtime, provided you get out of the kitchen and let me get it started," Rosie laughed again.

"Ya want ta stay an' eat with me?" Hezekiah looked hopeful.

"I'm not sure that's such a *gut* idea, Hezekiah. *Mamm* and *Dat* will worry when I don't show up at lunchtime."

"I'm goin' over ta look at wood with yer *Daed*, ta do some whittlin'. If'n he's okay with it, what do ya say?"

"Well, I guess," Rosie agreed hesitantly.

"I'll take Seth with me; that way ya can have the *haus* ta yerself."

Rosie looked down at Seth and smiled, recalling his rosy red cheeks when he had been outside with Hezekiah the week before.

"I'll take *gut* care of him," Hezekiah promised, hoping to sway Rosie's indecision.

"All right, but if he gets cold, take him in and leave him with *Mamm*."

"I'll do that. Scout's honor," Hezekiah saluted.

"How do you know about Boy Scouts?" Rosie asked, intrigued.

"That's telling all," Hezekiah teased. Realizing he didn't want to dissuade her interest, he amended. "When I was away, I helped out with a group of Scouts, teachin' them how to tie knots and build a *gut* campfire. Sometimes, we took the boys out campin'."

"That sounds like so much fun. You must have enjoyed it."

"*Ja*. I did. Leadin' a group of boys was one of the things I enjoyed most when I was away."

"I wish I had such *gut* memories," Rosie sighed. "*Kumme*, I'll get Seth dressed if he's going with you."

"Do ya mind if'n I use yer family buggy? My open buggy might be too cold fer, my little Buddy, here."

Warmth seeped into Rosie's smile at Hezekiah, calling Seth his little buddy. "*Ja*. For certain. But tell *Dat*, or he'll think you've done me in and taken off with the buggy," she laughed, thinking it was funny.

Hezekiah scowled. "Ya know, I'd never do that, Rosie. Not ever. Ya mean the whole world ta me. But I will let yer *Daed* know I'm borrowin' the buggy 'cause it's closed in an' it's warmer fer Seth."

Rosie looked at him, alarmed. She had meant it as a joke, but he had taken her seriously. Nodding, she turned to place the chicken in a large bowl. Hearing the outside door click when Hezekiah closed it softly, Rosie dashed away a tear. 'Did Dennis brainwash me so well that I automatically assume all men are like him? Consciously, or subconsciously?' She heaved a great sigh, lifting a prayer heavenward. 'Please, *Gott*. I don't want to live like this for the rest of my life. Can You please help me?' She glanced down and sighed again as Seth scribbled in the coloring book. Hezekiah would be around with the horse and buggy soon. Quickly, she busied herself dressing Seth.

He squirmed and looked about, making it difficult for her to put his winter clothes on him.

Hezekiah opened the door, and Seth went to him immediately. No coaxing was required. He was ready to go.

"I'll keep him warm." Hezekiah picked Seth up, "And I'll tell yer *Daed* I haven't kidnapped ya, so he won't worry."

At Rosie's flushed cheeks, he chuckled. "At least not yet, but one day," he challenged, laughing as he went out the door - Seth in his arms.

Rosie stood at the kitchen window and waved to Seth. He was wreathed in smiles as he looked up at Hezekiah. Hezekiah pointed toward the house, and Seth followed his direction. They waved to her, and then they were gone.

Rosie hurried about the kitchen. She rinsed the bird inside and out, rubbed it with salt, and placed it in a deep pot of scalding water. Then a chopped onion and seasoning were dumped in with the chicken. Before long, the cooking smells in the kitchen permeated the rest of the house. Deciding a carrot would add flavor, Rosie finely chopped one and added it to the pot. Her Wednesday routine had always been to clean and tidy downstairs first. Today, she headed for the second floor first; that way, she would be in the kitchen to keep an eye on the cooking bird.

'I have to admit,' she thought as she dusted and mopped through the bedrooms. 'I can clean through the *haus* much faster when Hezekiah has Seth.' She stopped the dustcloth in mid-air. 'What a terrible thing to think. If it wasn't for Seth, I might not be here today. I only called

Dat, so he would get Seth because I couldn't look after him.'

The two hours flew by. Rosie had just finished mixing the batter for dumplings when the sound of boots stomping on the porch caused her to glance at the clock on the wall. 'They're home already!?'

Hezekiah opened the door and set Seth inside the door. "Mmm. Mmm. It sure smells *gut* in here. I'm goin' ta put the horse up, an' then I'll be right back." With that, he closed the door and was gone.

Rosie knelt before Seth and began removing his outside clothes. "Did you have fun?" She chatted away to her little boy. He never answered, but she never gave up hope that he would someday. Hearing Hezekiah on the side porch, Rosie dropped the dough into the thick stew. Seth must have heard him too. He was smiling and waiting at the door when Hezekiah opened it.

Hezekiah immediately scooped him up.

"He heard you on the porch and went over to meet you," Rosie informed.

"I was wonderin' if he had problems with his hearin' since he doesn't talk much," Hezekiah pondered.

"That's not why he doesn't talk," Rosie revealed, sadness creeping into her voice. "He was never allowed to make baby noises. It was…." She searched for an appropriate word and finally murmured, "Discouraged."

Rosie didn't see Hezekiah's eyes squint or his jaw clench. Deceptively quiet over her comment, he remarked, "Then we'll have ta change that, won't we, Buddy?" He addressed Seth, "*Kumme* on, Buddy." Hezekiah helped Seth wash his hands at the sink. "It's time ta eat." While they washed up, Rosie began ladling the thick stew into large bowls deciding to leave the dumplings. 'They can stand to cook a little longer,' she decided.

Hezekiah said the grace, though not the usual silent grace Rosie was accustomed to. His words were thanksgiving for the food in front of them and the health each one enjoyed. Lastly, he asked God to bless each one at the table, then ended the grace with a hearty, "Amen!" That amen was so familiar to Rosie. Her dad always ended their silent prayer at home in such a manner.

Rosie handed the bread to Hezekiah across the narrow table. He placed a slice beside Seth's bowl, then gave it back to her before taking a portion himself. Next, Hezekiah lathered his bread and Seth's with butter. Taking a minute, he cut the little boy's dumpling into mouth-sized pieces before digging into the food in his bowl. Seth picked up the spoon and dipped it in the food in his bowl as Rosie leaned over to assist him.

Hezekiah looked at her. "He can feed himself, Rosie."

Rosie returned his look; it offended her that Hezekiah would tell her what to do with her own child. "I've always fed him. Otherwise, he won't eat."

Hezekiah shrugged, not wishing to put a damper on their relationship. "Then ya should see him polish off a plate at the Meetin's," and resumed eating his stew.

Rosie sat back and watched Seth as he concentrated on getting the spoon from the bowl to his mouth. Realizing there was no need to make a mountain out of a molehill, she looked over at Hezekiah, wondering what she should say to get them back onto amiable ground.

As it was, Hezekiah seeing her indecision, remarked, "This is some *gut* stew, Rosie." Finishing the last bit in his bowl, "Is there enough fer seconds?" Not waiting for an answer, he went to the stove and helped himself. Noticing her stillness, he asked, "Are ya not eatin', Rosie? It's some *gut* food yer missin' out on. Even Seth is about finished."

Rosie, baffled, looked from Hezekiah over to Seth. 'Does he have some ulterior motive for being so nice all the time?' She thought waspishly, then corrected herself, 'That's not fair, Rosie; Hezekiah has always been nice to you.'

"Here, have this bowl," Hezekiah placed his refreshed bowl in front of her and took her bowl for himself. "Yers will be coolin' down."

Confused, Rosie blinked at him, her frown softening, and decided to change the topic. "Did you see *Dat*?"

"Yup. I told him I wouldn't kidnap ya. Not taday anyway."

"What did he say to that?" Rosie relaxed and smiled over at him.

"He said he'd know where ta *kumme* an' get ya, if'n I did."

Rosie smiled, grateful at Hezekiah's attempt to lighten the atmosphere. She glanced over at Seth. Seeing he was nearly finished, she concentrated on her chicken and dumplings.

"But I don't know. I might have ta go back on my word," Hezekiah chuckled. There's no way I could ever begin ta cook this *gut*," he motioned to his near-empty bowl. "*Danke*, Rosie."

"I'm glad you enjoyed it. Do you want dessert?"

"Dessert? Ya have dessert on top of this *gut* stew?"

When Rosie would have gotten up to get it for him, he insisted, "Sit down an' eat yer lunch, Rosie. I'm just goin' ta let things settle ta make room fer dessert. Ya want a little more, Buddy?" Taking Seth's bowl, he spooned a small amount into it. "This boy is a *gut* eater," he set the bowl before the child and watched as Seth dug into it.

"I've never seen him eat that much," Rosie watched with amazement.

"He's a growin' boy," Hezekiah smiled at the child.

Finished, Rosie carried the bowls to the sink. "*Kaffee*, Hezekiah?"

"I'll get it. Why don't ya get the dessert out fer us?" They sidestepped around one another until they were sitting once again. "I might be too full ta go back outside after lunch," Hezekiah informed Rosie between mouthfuls of apple crisp.

Rosie laughed. "I did say that, didn't I?"

Hezekiah moaned. "Yer not goin' ta hold me ta it, are ya?"

"I guess not this time," she smiled. Rosie surprised herself by thinking, 'It's so easy to be around Hezekiah.'

He sipped his coffee. "I won't be here next Wednesday."

"Oh?" Rosie looked at him wide-eyed.

"*Dat* an' me are takin' a load of calves ta Kitchener. Do ya want ta *kumme* on Tuesday or Thursday instead?"

"*Ja*. Tuesday would be better. Esther and I are making a quilt to sell at the store in town, and I go to her *haus* Thursday mornings."

"Are ya now?" He crossed his arms over his chest, and a grin lit up his face. "Esther Kuepfer is a nice friend ta have."

"*Ja*. We've known each other all our lives."

"Like you an' me have, all our lives."

"I guess we have, haven't we?" Rosie smiled.

"Yup. An' like we're goin' ta fer the rest of our lives." He didn't wait for Rosie to respond but stood and carried the dishes to the sink. "Do ya want help doin' up the dishes?"

Rosie looked stunned at his offer, then quickly recovered enough to respond, "*Nee*. I can wash them up in no time."

"Then I'm goin' ta put my feet up an' let all that *gut* food digest."

Rosie watched him lay down on the couch. No sooner had he lay his head back on the couch's armrest than Seth climbed up and lay beside him.

"Ooff, mind my stomach, Buddy. It's some full."

She smiled at their coziness and turned back to tidy the kitchen. A half-hour later, a sleepy voice asked. "Will I tell yer folks yer goin' ta stay here with me?"

"Not this time," she smiled at him, calling his bluff.

"Ah ha, that's a change," he raised his eyebrows. "Then someday, ya might just say, *Ja*."

"*Ja*. When there's a blue moon in the sky!" Rosie laughed.

"Oww. That hurts. In the meantime, I'll be lookin' fer that blue moon, an' when I see it, I'll be holdin' ya ta yer word." He smiled crookedly at her and rolled to a sitting position, cradling Seth as he did so. "I'll go get yer horse ready, seen as I can't change yer mind right now. I'll see ya at Sunday Meetin'?" At Rosie's nod, he added, "I'll keep an eye on Seth fer ya, an' afterward, I can drive ya home to have his afternoon rest." He looked down at the sleeping child, "Ahh, ta be young again." He stood up, pulled his jacket on, and settled his black felt hat on his head. "Give me ten minutes, an' I'll *kumme* in an' carry Seth out fer ya."

"*Danke*," Rosie returned and packed their bag, ready to leave. When Hezekiah pulled the horse up, she placed Seth's arms in his jacket, wiggled his feet into his boots, his hands into his mitts, and wrapped a scarf around his face. As Hezekiah opened the door, she settled her cape over her shoulders.

"Are ya ready ta go?" He stepped into the kitchen.

"*Ja*," she nodded and looked around the kitchen one last time. Turning, she was surprised to find Hezekiah watching her, an intense look in his eyes.

"I enjoyed havin' you an' Seth stay ta have lunch with me."

"Me too," Rosie admitted.

"*Kumme*," he leaned over. "I'll carry our boy out fer ya," He picked up the sleeping Seth. Hezekiah saw them settled in the buggy and tucked the carriage robe about them. Bidding her, "Drive safe." He stepped back as the horse pulled away.

As she drove home, Rosie could only think about how gentle and caring Hezekiah had been. She had not missed him referring to Seth as "our boy." No one had ever thought of Seth that way; for certain, Dennis hadn't. That man could never hold a candle to Hezekiah - not in a million years.

Tobiah met her at the barn and carried his sleeping grandson to the house. "I see Hezekiah didn't kidnap ya," he grinned mischievously at her.

"Not today, anyway, *Dat*," Rosie responded, her grin mirroring his.

Tobiah chuckled at her comeback and lay the sleeping child on the couch, then hurried back to the barn to take care of the horse.

~ ~ ~

And be kind and compassionate to one another…
~ Ephesians 4:32 ~

Chapter 11

Graciousness and Healing

The weeks tripped along, drifting everyone closer to Christmas. Rosie and Seth made their weekly trip unless the weather was too snowy or cold. During those weeks, stuck a home, Seth was irritable and inconsolable, often climbing a chair to keep watch out the window. It broke Rosie's heart to see him call "Mama" repeatedly. Hezekiah heard about Seth's distress and made a special trip to visit him. He spent a couple of hours holding the little boy while talking with Tobiah. Every time he visited, a meal was in the offering before he needed to return and feed his calves.

Rosie stopped taking Hezekiah seriously when he teased. A camaraderie found a way into their hearts, bonded by a common interest to nurture Seth. She realized if she wanted to take their friendship to the next level, Hezekiah would have been only too willing. But it seemed he desired to respect her wishes, happy with the mutual bond developing between them.

On her regular trip to Hezekiah's, the Wednesday before Christmas, Rosie cut some evergreen boughs, nestled them across the hearth, and added cedar sprigs and red holly berries on the side cupboard. In the windows, she arranged cedar branches and tucked in a few holly berries, completing the window dressing by placing a candle in the center. The kitchen's warmth made the cedar and pine release their homey smell, filling the kitchen with the scent of warm evergreen. Hezekiah, coming into the kitchen, breathed long and deep. "That's one of the best smells at this time of year. It's clean an' smells of the bush after cuttin' down trees fer firewood." He smiled at Rosie and gave a nod of satisfaction. "Them man-made smells don't even *kumme* close. *Danke* Rosie, fer bringin' some of the outdoors inside."

Rosie returned his smile, happy she could make the kitchen smell so good with little or no effort simply by cutting and arranging a few cedar and pine boughs.

~.~.~.~

Christmas morning dawned bright and crisp; newly fallen snow had blotted out the tracks from the day before. The only tracks evident was Tobiah's going to the barn to do chores, plus those of snowshoe rabbits crisscrossing back and forth across the yard.

Hearing Tobiah stomping snow from his boots, Miriam and Rosie hurried to get Christmas breakfast on the table. He opened the door and exclaimed, "Looks like we had an early mornin' visitor." In one arm, he carried a dozen roses; in the other, a dappled grey wooden horse on red rockers.

The first words out of Seth's mouth were, "Mama!" Toddling over, he wrapped chubby arms around the rocking horse's neck.

"Since the rockin' horse is fer Seth, I guess these must be fer ya," Tobiah handed the flowers to Rosie.

Rosie stared at them, dumbfounded. Tears formed in her astonished eyes and clung to her eyelashes as she blinked rapidly.

"*Ach* Rosie, they're lovely," Miriam exclaimed. She hurried to pull an empty canning jar from the pantry shelf and fill it with water.

"Did you see anyone out there?" Rosie looked at her dad.

"*Nee*, but these were put on the porch within the last half hour 'cause they weren't out there when I went ta do chores."

Rosie unwrapped a bouquet of beautiful red roses accented by delicate white Baby's Breath. Long trembling fingers opened a tiny envelope tucked between the long stems. "Merry Christmas to my sweet, sweet Rosie," was written in bold handwriting. No signature followed those few endearing words. Then again, none were needed, for Rosie knew who had brought them without a shadow of a doubt. The same person that had given her a rose years ago, subjecting himself to teasing from the other boys at school. Tears splashed down onto the roses, and she blinked furiously, gulping, trying to get control of her emotions.

Her dear sweet mother came to the rescue. "Let's put them on the table," Miriam suggested, and that is where they sat for the duration of Christmas day. They were a touching reminder that Hezekiah had not and would not forget her - his first and only love.

Realization dawned on Rosie that she needed to talk to him one day and one day very soon. He needed to know she could not and would not allow herself to be dominated by another man ever again. She owed it to herself, she owed it to Seth, and she most definitely owed an explanation to Hezekiah. It wasn't fair that she lead him on. Rosie knew he would wait for her forever. He was that kind of guy, but there was no future for them together, ever, as far as she was concerned.

The opportunity came sooner than she expected, on her regular cleaning day, right after Christmas. Hezekiah met them and took the horse and sleigh to the barn. His thoughtfulness allowed her and Seth to trek along the path, through the snow, to the house. She knew he would come to the house before she started the cleaning. It had become a routine with them to chat for a few minutes over coffee before he returned to the barn. It gave everyone a chance to warm up; Rosie, after driving through the cold, and Hezekiah from tending the stock. Seth sat with them at the table, enjoying hot chocolate.

Hezekiah set his coffee cup on the table and looked at Rosie. "Rosie, won't ya consider movin' here with me an' bein' my *frau*? I'd be *gut* ta ya, Rosie, an' a *gut daed* ta Seth." He took her hands and held them lightly, thumbs caressing her fingers.

Rosie gulped. 'This is the moment I've been waiting for, but how to put it into words.'
"Hezekiah, I can't," she saw the hesitation in his eyes as he stared back at her. "I promised myself I'd never give any *mann* the power to tell me what to do, ever again. Besides, I'm not like I was before I went away; I've changed," her eyes pleaded with him to understand.

He continued holding her hands. "When ya went away, one week later, I left too. Not on *rumspringa* like everybody thinks, but ta look fer ya. I looked fer ya fer over a year, Rosie. Then, *Gott* told me ta *kumme* home. So, I did. I bought this place with you in mind that you would have someplace ta *kumme* home ta, if'n ya needed a place." He looked around the room, taking in the personal touches she'd added. "This is yer home, Rosie. I bought it fer ya. As far as ya changin', ya haven't. Ta me yer still, my Rosie. Some guy took what he had no right takin'. I've loved ya all my life, Rosie. And I will fer the rest of our lives. Don't ya see, you an' Seth belong here with me?"

"I just can't let another *mann* tell me what I should or shouldn't be doing," Rosie insisted unhappily.

"And I won't. Ours will be a partnership, Rose. Not me forcin' ya ta do what ya don't want ta do. How do ya think a *mann*, a real *mann*, should act or feel fer that matter? I ain't like this other guy, forcin' himself on ya. He held ya against yer will, forcin' ya ta be with him and wouldn't feed ya or Seth. I'm not offerin' ya that, Rosie. I want ta love an' protect ya fer the rest of our lives. My intentions are honorable, Rosie." He caressed her fingers before gently letting her hands go. He leaned forward, kissed her fleetingly on the cheek, then left the house.

Rosie sat stunned and placed a hand on her cheek where he'd kissed her. She batted her eyelashes, attempting to stem back the tears. Seth slid off his chair and laid his head on her lap, and she held him close. "*Kumme*," she whispered, a sad sob shuddered through her body. "I better get the *haus* cleaned so we can go home."

'Well, I did it! All that time planning my words, but rather than feeling relief, I feel like I've ruined everything.' Giving a great sigh of sadness, she turned her eyes heavenward. 'Whatever You want for Seth and me, I trust You, *Gott*.' She tidied the house, but her heart wasn't in it today.

Two hours later, Hezekiah poked his head in the door. "I'll get the horse ready if'n yer near ready ta leave."

"*Ja*. In about ten or fifteen minutes," she nodded. She had placed a small roast surrounded by vegetables in the oven. "I'll check your lunch, and we'll be right out."

"It sure smells *gut* in here. Are ya sure ya won't stay an' eat with me?"

"Maybe not this time, but I'll let Mamm know I might be a little later next week." She smiled at his look of anticipation of them eating with him again. "Do you want to eat supper with us tonight?" The words slipped out of her mouth as if her heart had a mind of its own. She bit her bottom lip, wondering what she'd just gotten herself into.

"Fer sure?" At Rosie's nod of affirmation added, "Can I bring anything?"

"A healthy appetite?" Rosie smiled, unable to keep a straight face.

"Ya don't have ta worry about my appetite. It's always healthy." He grinned back at her, glad they were back on better footing. "Is six-ish *gut*? It'll give me time ta get my chores outa the way before *kummin'* over."

"Six is *gut*," Rosie assured him.

He closed the door behind him and went to the barn to harness the horse and put it into the cutter. If anyone had been watching him, they would have noticed his step had suddenly become lighter.

When she was alone, Rosie looked heavenward. '*Danke* for getting us back to being friends, *Gott*. I don't know

how I could face another day if we weren't friends.'
Involuntary tears fell from her eyes. She swiped at them
with the back of her hand and opened the oven to check on
the roast. Another half hour and it would be ready for
Hezekiah's lunch.

"*Kumme*," she held her hand out to Seth. "We need to
pack our things. It's time to go home." Rosie continued
chatting while placing his little arms in the sleeves of his
jacket. A twinge in her newly healed arm pulled her back
to that terrifying day and the nauseating pain. 'If I hadn't
stopped Dennis, it could have been Seth's little arm that
was broken instead of mine.' Recalling caused her to break
out in a cold sweat, and the unwelcome thoughts sucked
her back to a time in her life she wished she could forget.
Rosie shook her head, trying to dispel the vivid images of
that terrible day and the lies she'd told to protect Dennis
from being arrested. His words to the nurse at the hospital
still rang in her ears, as clearly as if it had just happened,
"Ah, she wasn't careful and slipped goin' down the steps."

Later, when she was in the emergency room alone with
the nurse, the woman asked, "Rose, how did you get all
these bruises?"

She had answered as calmly as she could. "Probably
from falling."

The nurse had looked at her closely, but Rosie couldn't
look her in the eye, and nothing more came of it.

Now, here was Hezekiah asking her to trust him. If he
only knew what she'd been through and how hard it would
be for her to trust another man.

Hezekiah returned to the house to carry Seth to the
cutter. He saw them settled safely in the sleigh, then

tucked the lap robe carefully around them. Stepping back, he reminded, "I'll see ya around six."

"*Gut*, we'll see you then," Rosie smiled. "Don't forget the pot roast will be ready in about ten minutes for your lunch."

"I'll not be fergettin'," he smiled, laughter in his eyes. "An' I'm not fergettin' somethin' else, either."

Rosie looked at him, puzzled. If it had been Dennis telling her he wouldn't forget, it would have come across as a threat, but from Hezekiah, it came across as a pleasant promise meant to make her laugh, which she did.

"I'm still waitin' on that blue moon in the sky."

Rosie smiled broadly, finding it funny he was willing to put fate in the moon's color. "You might be waiting a long time," she tossed back at him.

"We'll see," his eyes laughed into hers. "My *Mamm* says, he who laughs first, laughs last. That means he who laughs last laughs best." He raised his hand in farewell as Rosie clucked to the horse to move forward.

All the way home, Rosie thought about that phrase. 'What if he ever did *kumme* up with a blue moon? Well then, ya better 'fess up, Rosie girl,' she thought ironically. 'Would I let him hold me to my word?' Deep down, Rosie knew it would be a way for her to give in graciously. Then a series of thoughts flicked through her mind. 'You know you enjoy doing for him and being near him. Why are you playing so hard to catch?'

Rosie's natural survival instinct began coming up with all kinds of excuses. But, Scrooge's words, "Bah, humbug," put a stop to her excuses. Instead, she toyed with the idea of being married to Hezekiah and what it would mean for Seth as well. Even though it was cold out, once again, within a short period of time, she broke out into a cold sweat at the idea of allowing another to have a say in her life. The idea that she would go willingly into another relationship was very frightening. Pulling the horse up to the barn put an end to her errant thoughts, the could have's, would have's, and should have's. She smiled when her dad came from the barn and tied the horse to a hitching ring on the barn before carrying Seth to the house.

"How did yer mornin' go?" Tobiah asked as they made their way to the house.

"Really *gut, Dat*. Hezekiah is *kumming* for supper."

"Is he now? *Gut*, I've been wantin' ta ask him, next time he goes ta Kitchener ta look out fer another horse fer us. It seems we've been *kummin'* up short lately of a *gut* driver. Better still, it might be best if'n I went with him an' had a look-see fer myself."

~ ~ ~

Gracious words are a honeycomb,
sweet to the soul and healing to the bones
~ Proverbs 16:24 ~

Chapter 12

Let Not Your Hearts be Troubled

Hezekiah was as good as his word; just before six, he arrived in his one-horse open sleigh. It was a clear, crisp night, with a moon as big as a harvest moon rising in the sky. Tobiah shrugged into his coat and grabbed a lantern, making his way out to help the younger man undo straps and settle the horse in the barn.

"Seth, *kumme*." Rosie lifted her son so that he could look out the window. "Look who's *kumme* to visit us." Seth planted his nose against the window and peered through the frost-covered pane of glass. He turned and looked at Rosie, his eyes alive, a smile lighting up his face. "Mama?" He whispered, full of hope and wonder.

Rosie nodded her head. "*Ja*. He's going to have supper with us." When Seth would have scrambled down from the chair, Rosie detained him. "Wait here; that way, we can see him when he *kummes* with *Dawdi* from the barn." They both waited, a pair of noses pressed against the window.

Miriam chuckled to herself. 'That's the most excited I've seen Rosie since she's been home.' She turned to the stove and mashed the potatoes. 'Maybe Tobiah's right, and maybe Hezekiah is what our *tochter* needs.' Dumping in a large dollop of butter and seasoning the potatoes with salt and pepper, she remembered, 'If Rosie is right, and he has a healthy appetite, we'll need lots of food.'

While Seth slept the afternoon away, Miriam and Rosie had made two large meatloaves. They'd scrubbed and boiled potatoes in their jackets, peeled carrots, and cut up a turnip to boil. The house smelled delicious. Tobiah put his stamp of approval on all the food they'd prepared for their guest, helping himself to samples when Miriam wasn't looking. Rosie finished the meal prep by cutting the leftover Christmas mincemeat pie into slices.

Miriam smiled, remembering the fun they had, pulling the meal together. Seth's excited "Mama" forewarned Miriam the men were approaching the house. "*Kumme* give me a hand, would you, Rosie? There's still the turnips to mash, and we need to put the *kaffee* to perking."

"*Ja, Mamm*," Rosie responded, distracted, setting an excited Seth on the floor.

No sooner had Hezekiah stepped through the door than Seth was all over him. He jumped up and down in excitement, not giving Hezekiah a chance to shrug out of his jacket. Kneeling before the little boy, he looked up at Rosie. "Wasn't it only this mornin' ya were over at my place?" He smiled broadly. "Seth acts like he hasn't seen me in days." He stood up, lifting the little boy as he did so.

"I guess you're pretty high on his list of important people," Rosie smiled. "Let me take him so you can take your coat off."

"I'll get him, Rose," Tobiah assured. "Go ahead and help yer *Mamm*."

Hezekiah nodded toward Miriam. "It sure smells *gut* in here, just like when Rosie pulls a meal tagether fer me. I keep askin' her ta stay, but I ain't had much luck so far," his booming laughter filled the kitchen. Miriam and

Tobiah exchanged amused looks and joined in his infectious mood.

Rosie crimsoned. She mashed the turnips with more enthusiasm than necessary to hide her embarrassment. Sprinkling in a little brown sugar, she added butter and seasoning before dumping the mixture into a bowl.

"*Kumme* and wash up," Miriam invited. "We'll go ahead and eat while everything's hot." When the men had taken seats at the table, Seth pulled himself up on a chair beside Hezekiah. "Looks like we need ta put some books on the chair fer, my little Buddy, here," Hezekiah looked from Seth to Tobiah.

"He has a highchair," Rosie intervened.

Tobiah took the matter out of everyone's hands and got up from the table. "*Frau*, where are those booster seats I made fer the girls when they were small?"

Miriam smiled. "Look in the pantry; I use them to step on when I can't reach something on the top shelf."

Minutes later, the women set the food on the table and sat down while Hezekiah lifted Seth from the chair, and Tobiah slid the riser onto the seat. "That's better. Now yer one of the men," Hezekiah smiled at the little boy.

Seth looked at everyone at the table, a pleased grin plastered across his face.

Following the offering, and as everyone helped themselves, Miriam watched Seth, surprised. "I didn't know he fed himself."

"*Ja*, given half the chance, he'd probably do a lot more, too," Tobiah mumbled between mouthfuls.

Miriam looked at him sharply, then over at Rosie's wilted look, and quickly changed the subject. "Are you taking another bunch of your calves to Kitchener soon?" She broached the subject, knowing Tobiah had wanted to look for another horse.

Tobiah nodded, grateful she had a good memory, maybe sometimes too good in his estimation. Glancing at Rosie's withdrawn expression, he was doubly thankful for Miriam's excellent timing.

"*Ja*. In a couple of weeks. This meatloaf is some *gut*," Hezekiah relished another forkful without looking up.

"Rosie made it," Miriam informed him and helped herself to another slice.

Hezekiah looked appreciatively over at Rosie and smiled at her flushed cheeks.

Tobiah saw an opportunity to redeem his thoughtless words and nodded toward his daughter, "That's our Rosie; she really knows how to whip up a meal. I never go away from her cookin', hungry."

Miriam's, "How's Seth doing?" Redirected everyone's attention back to the table.

Rosie smiled at Seth, "He's certainly got a *gut* appetite."

Hezekiah glanced down at the child and chuckled. "*Das gut*. We gotta build them muscles up."

"We're needin' another driver. How's the selection at Kitchener?" Tobiah asked.

"Like everything else. If'n ya take yer time an' look everything over, ya can find something. Ya want to go next time *Dat* an' me go?"

"*Ja*. If'n ya got enough room."

"We pay someone ta follow the stock truck, so there's always room. We get away early so's I can make sure the calves get weighed in an' settled with a little water."

"*Das gut*. It'll be a day out," Tobiah nodded, satisfied. "I'll check an' see if'n Jed Kuepfer wants ta get away fer the day."

"Sounds *gut*. There's plenty of room in the van," Hezekiah's concentration returned to his plate of food.

After the meal, Rosie and Miriam tidied the kitchen. The men remained sitting at the table, talking shop and drinking coffee. Seth, fighting valiantly to stay awake, climbed onto Hezekiah's lap, but the odds were against him. With a full stomach and feeling secure, he leaned back against Hezekiah's chest and fell asleep.

Kitchen chores behind them, Rosie offered. "I'll take him upstairs and put him to bed."

"I'll carry him, Rose," Hezekiah stood up, cradling the sleeping child.

Rosie glanced at her dad, wondering how appropriate it would be to go upstairs alone with Hezekiah.

"We'll have pie an' *kaffee* when ya get back down," Tobiah informed them and padded over to the sideboard to bring the coffee mugs to the table.

After Rosie and Hezekiah, carrying Seth, disappeared upstairs, Miriam murmured to Tobiah. "Is that wise, having them go upstairs together?"

"Are ya hidin' somethin' up there that ya don't want others ta see, *frau*?" Tobiah chuckled at her exasperated look. "They're *gut*; I expect they'll be married come this time next year anyway."   Miriam looked at him and sputtered.

"That's a first, ain't?" Tobiah smiled mischievously. "Not havin' somethin' ta say."

Miriam threw him a look that spoke volumes, causing Tobiah to chuckle, amused.

Upstairs, Rosie quickly turned the covers down in Seth's crib and pulled the child's pants off before Hezekiah settled him onto the bed.

Noticing Hezekiah glancing at her bed and then Seth's crib, Rosie murmured, "I know he needs his own room. I just haven't got around to it, that's all."

"If'n ya give him a single bed when ya move him ta another room, he'll go easier. It'll make him feel all grown up."

Rosie heaved a sigh and shrugged.

"Are ya havin' a hard time lettin' him grow up, Rosie?" He looked at her sympathetically.

"*Ja*," she admitted, "It's just, there have been so many changes in the last six months."

"Ya can't keep livin' in the past, ya know. It ain't *gut* fer Seth an' it ain't *gut* fer ya, either. That person ain't goin' ta do nothin' ta either of ya anymore." At Rosie's worried frown, he assured, "Do ya honestly think anyone in our order would let him walk in an' take you or Seth away? All I can say is let 'em try. We're peaceful people, but even we have our limits, Rosie. *Kumme*," he stood at the door. "I'll have that pie an' *kaffee* yer *daed* was talkin' about, then get on my way." They descended the steps together. The aroma of freshly perked coffee greeted them as they entered the kitchen. They sipped their coffee, ate liberal servings of mincemeat pie, and made small talk.

"I hope ya can see ta make yer way home safely," Tobiah commented, concerned.

"There was a big *alt* moon *kummin'* up when I came over earlier. It was almost as bright as a Harvest moon!" Hezekiah chuckled.

Rosie and Miriam stood near the door as Hezekiah and Tobiah pulled on coats and stepped into warm boots.

"*Danke*, I had a real nice evenin'." Hezekiah offered his appreciation, bobbed his head, and stepped onto the porch.

Tobiah followed closely so the cold air wouldn't slip in, causing the house to cool. "I'll check the stock, then be right back," he assured the women before closing the door. They made the short trek to the barn, snow crunching underfoot.

"That's one interestin' lookin' moon *tanacht*," Tobiah remarked. "I expect it's because we're supposed ta have somethin' they call a lunar eclipse."

Hezekiah stopped and followed Tobiah's gaze. "Would ya say that moon looks blue?" Hezekiah asked, astounded.

"*Ja*. About as blue as they get…" Tobiah's voice petered off. Dumfounded, his eyes followed Hezekiah as the younger man suddenly ran back toward the house. "What on earth?" Tobiah mumbled and followed their visitor.

Hezekiah threw open the door with a huge smile plastered on his face. "Rosie, *kumme*. I got somethin' ta show ya." He snatched a cape off the peg beside the door and held it open for her.

By this time, Tobiah had joined them, a stupefied look on his face.

Hezekiah turned and said to him. "Ya need ta *kumme* back outside with us. I ain't havin' Rosie see this on my say so." He eagerly led a baffled Rosie away from the house so she could get the full benefit of the moon. "Rosie, what do ya see?" He asked, uncensored delight in his voice.

"I don't know what you mean, Hezekiah," she looked at him, baffled.

"See that moon, Rosie?" He pointed to the moon for her benefit.

Rosie looked at the moon, floored. With her lips pursed together, she nodded mutely.

"Wouldn't ya say that is about the bluest moon ya has ever seen, Rosie?" Hezekiah beamed with joy.

She looked from the moon to Hezekiah and back again, licking her lips nervously. "*Ja*. It's blue," she finally agreed in a small voice.

"So ya agree it's blue?" Hezekiah asked again, waiting with bated breath for her answer.

"*Ja*," she nodded hesitantly. She wondered how to get out of the promise she'd made to him, but more so, did she really want to.

"An' ya agree. It's blue," Hezekiah asked Tobiah.

"*Ja*. I've never seen a moon exactly that color before. But it's blue, alright," Tobiah agreed.

Miriam walked up behind them. "It's beautiful; it's one of *Gott's* wonders, ain't so?"

Hezekiah whooped, unable to contain his joy one second longer. With no effort, he picked Rosie up and swung her around.

She couldn't help but giggle. "Hezekiah! Put me down!" She demanded while laughing.

He did so and gave her a sound kiss on the cheek. "Ya just made me the happiest *mann* on earth," then scooping her up, carried her to the porch. "*Guten nacht*, my sweet Rosie," he set her safely on the porch. Laughing loudly, he turned and headed back toward the barn.

Tobiah didn't ask what was uppermost on his and Miriam's minds. But he planned on returning to the house as soon as possible to hear Rosie's side. He saw Hezekiah off and hurried toward the house, forgetting to check the livestock; he didn't want Rosie taking off upstairs before he heard her explanation of Hezekiah's behavior.

Miriam looked up, shocked as he entered the kitchen. "You're back quick."

He removed his hat and kicked off his boots before entering the room. "*Ja*. I want ta hear what Rosie has to say about why Hezekiah is so happy about that moon."

Miriam began, "Well,.."

Tobiah held up his hand toward her. "*Nee*! It's Rosie's say." He waited, not so patiently, with eyebrows raised, waiting for Rosie to go on.

"Well,…"

"*Ja*. Yer *Mamm* started fer ya, now all ya need do is finish," he urged.

Rosie licked her lips nervously and looked at her mother. "Ya know how Hezekiah has been teasing and saying he wants me to move in with him…"

"Uh-huh!" An impatient look crossed Tobiah's face. "What has that got ta do with the moon?" Tobiah frowned, his voice raising an octave.

"Well,.." Rosie began, and her dad nodded as if to say, 'So, go on.' "Well,.. I told him when there was a blue moon in the sky. But I only meant it in jest, but he told me he'd be looking for that blue moon and hold me to my word."

Tobiah roared, laughing, and Miriam shook her head, having difficulty keeping a straight face. "Shh," she warned Tobiah. "Or you'll wake Seth."

"So, now what will I do?" Rosie looked imploringly at her parents.

"Be honorable and stand by yer word," Tobiah slapped his hat on his head. "This is the best laugh I've had in a long time." He left the house and headed to the barn, still chuckling.

"I guess you're getting married," Miriam smiled, pleased. At Rosie's hopeless look, she offered, "Hezekiah will be a *wunderbar gut mann* to you, Rosie."

"But I promised myself I'd never let another *mann* tell me what to do."

"I can't imagine Hezekiah telling you what to do - consulting and talking things over. *Ja.* But bossing you? *Nee.* I don't see that. Do ya have no feelings for him at all?"

"*Ja.* But I'm kind of afraid too."

"That's natural, especially after what's happened to you. Hezekiah thinks the whole world of you, Rosie. Can't you give him a chance?"

"I guess the matter's out of my hands, thanks to that dumb moon being blue," she grumbled.

Miriam chuckled, "Next time, don't make promises so rashly. Especially ones you don't want to keep. But maybe deep down you do, huh?" She smiled kindly at Rosie.

Rosie blushed. "I know Hezekiah will be *gut* to Seth and me."

"So?" Her mother looked at her.

"So. Can you help me with what I should do next?"

"*Ja*. I'll talk to your *Daed*. You didn't get baptized before you went on *rumspringa*. I expect you'll have to go through the baptismal classes. But it's not impossible. Then, you and Hezekiah better speak to the Bishop for the next season. You have the better part of a year before the wedding season *kummes* again next fall. Without waiting for Rosie to comment, Miriam prattled on. "Then we need to get your wedding dress sewn." She recalled helping Ruthie and Rachel before their weddings. Beaming at Rosie, she said, "This is how I always planned it- to help you with your wedding. Now, it's *kumming* true." She blinked back happy tears that suddenly threatened to flow.

Rosie hugged her mom. "*Ja*. Now it's *kumming* true. Did you know Hezekiah liked me when we were *kinder*?"

"*Ja*, but you weren't too happy about it at the time. All you saw was a little boy that teased you all the time. He's not unlike your *Daed*, you know. Your *Daed's* a terrible tease, but he's been *gut* to me and you girls. I don't believe I'd be happy with an *alt* stick in the mud. *Gott* knows who we are best suited to, and Hezekiah is who He has picked for you. So, relax and enjoy one another and let *Gott* do the rest."

"*Danke Mamm*. Said like that, it makes a lot of sense. I think tomorrow I'll put Seth over in Ruthie's *alt* room. Hezekiah said something tonight that made sense." At her mother's look of inquiry, she added, "He said I wasn't letting Seth grow up because of my insecurities." She shrugged. "So, I guess I need to let go a little bit," she smiled.

Miriam smiled. "We can take the crib down. Is it something you want Hezekiah here for?" At Rosie's frown, she added. "Do all things together - talk together, cry together, work together, play together and pray together. It'll make your marriage stronger."

Rosie nodded. "I'll go to Hezekiah's and ask him if he can spare some time tomorrow. I know he'll be pleased to be a part of it. Can you look after Seth while I drive over and ask him?"

"For certain. It all begins with just one small step. Ain't so?"

Rosie nodded, smiling at her mother.

~ ~ ~

... Do not let your hearts be troubled and do not be afraid.
~ John 14:27 ~

Chapter 13
A Season for Miracles

Rosie drove to Hezekiah's farm with a light heart the following morning. The horse trotted along, seemingly as happy as she was. Perhaps it was also because he looked forward to seeing Hezekiah and the measure of grain that was always given to him. Regardless, Rose didn't have to worry about being lost in her daydream world because the horse knew exactly where he was going.

The horse suddenly jerked to one side, startled as Hezekiah barged out the kitchen door, effectively bringing Rosie back to reality.

"Everything alright, Rosie?" His eyebrows were drawn together, not understanding why she was there. Seeing she wasn't in immediate danger, the hot coffee registered as it sloshed out of the cup, and he quickly transferred it to his other hand.

"I was going to move Seth's bed across the hall from my room, and I wondered if you'd like to *kumme* and help. It might make the transition a happier event for Seth if you were there."

A slow, crooked grin replaced the scowl of worry. With a gleam in his eyes, he assured, "I wouldn't miss it fer the world. But first, *kumme*. Let's take a moment an' see what room ya think would be *gut* fer him here once we're married."

Rosie stared at him, surprised he was making plans already.

"Yer not backin' out on me, are ya, Rosie?" He looked at her, deflated.

She shook her head, unable to look at him. Rosie would be the first to admit that she was happy with how her life had turned around, but still, she felt a little overwhelmed and rushed.

"*Gut.* 'Cause I'd be awful disappointed; I just want to make ya happy." He smiled tenderly at her. "*Kumme*," he led the horse over and tied it to the tree. "We'll only be a few minutes an' the horse will be *gut, an'* then we can go back to yer parent's place tagether," He looked elated.

"Well, how will you get home?" She did look up at him then, confused.

"Ya wouldn't give yer betrothed a ride home, Rosie?" He teased. "Why don't you an' Seth bring me back? It'd be our first family outin'," he grinned.

Rosie looked at Hezekiah, a smile softening the lines of concern on her face. '*Mamm's* right. He is a lot like *Dat.*' Suddenly, she thought it funny and chuckled, "Are you going to be like this our whole lives?"

The scowl on his face returned, reminding her of Seth. "Like what, Rosie?"

"Teasing!"

"I don't tease!" His face became a study of concern. "I could change if'n I tried hard."

"It'll never happen - it's right in your blood. Besides, I wouldn't know how to take you if you were an *alt*, set in his ways, bachelor."

"Ahh," he looked at her, his mischievous smile returning. "But yer goin' ta make sure I ain't stayin' an *alt* bachelor, ain't so Rosie?"

"I guess the moon had a say in it," she grinned, enjoying their banter.

"Rosie, I've been waitin' fer this my whole life. The day ya'd say ya'd marry me. Ya will, won't ya, Rosie? Marry me?"

"*Ja*." She smiled at him sweetly.

He picked her up out of the cutter with no effort and carried her to the house, both laughing. Setting her carefully on the porch, Hezekiah gave Rosie a lingering kiss. "My sweet, sweet Rosie." He smiled and sighed, looking longingly into her blue eyes.

Rosie touched his face, her willingness to trust him shining in her eyes. She was willing to give her heart to this man who had loved her unconditionally for as long as she could remember.

"*Kumme*," his voice was husky with emotion, and he opened the door for her. "We better not linger. I don't want yer *Daed* ta think I kidnapped ya."

"He'd know where to find me if you did. Besides, maybe I don't want to go back." She smiled cheekily up at him.

He sputtered, taken aback, unsure how to respond.

"See. I can give it back as *gut* as you can give." Her face was a wreath of happy smiles.

"I can see we'll be havin' a real interesin' life, tagether." He chuckled.

"Don't get ahead of yourself; I'm not staying today. We have stuff to do, like moving a bed. Remember?"

They laughed together as their hearts bonded and climbed the steps to check out a suitable room for Seth.

~.~.~.~

Miriam, as promised, kept a close eye on Seth while Rosie was away. She gave him tiny carrots to chew on while she cut up vegetables to put in a stew with the leftover turkey from Christmas. And with some of that, she planned to make a turkey pot pie for supper. Glancing at the clock on the mantel, she realized Rosie and Hezekiah could return at any time, and she planned to have lunch ready when they did. Soon, all her girls would be married, but first, Rosie needed to go through the baptismal classes, all eighteen weeks of them. Tobiah had been right; by this time next year, Rosie and Hezekiah would be married. She smiled at the thought of another wedding being held in their home. A year would fly by, and then the daughter she thought she'd lost would be married and living close to home. Miriam smiled through happy tears and sent a prayer of thanksgiving heavenward. It would mean Seth would have a real dad who would encourage and love him, helping him grow into a responsible young Amish man.

Miriam peered over the table to see what her grandson was doing. It occurred to her that maybe, just maybe, she could get him to say something other than Mama. Most young children learn to say Da early, but how do I encourage him? Her opportunity came within minutes; Seth tiring of playing on his own, got up and began calling, "*Mama.*" Miriam dried her hands and picked him up before sitting in the rocker.

"*Mamma* has gone to get…" she hesitated, then added, "*Dat.*"

Seth looked at her; his nearness caused his eyes to rotate inward as he watched her mouth. "*Mama,*" he repeated.

"Dat," Miriam smiled, and for the next few minutes, they played their little game, Miriam patting his little hands together each time she said, "Dat." Finally, Miriam put the two words together. "Mama and Dat will be home for lunch soon."

"Daa," Seth repeated softly, almost as if he was afraid to say something other than Mama.

"Ja! That's gut!" Miriam clapped her hands in praise and gave him a big smile, hugging him before setting him on the floor.

As Seth's feet touched the floor, he ran to climb up on the chair and look out the window. "Mama," he smiled, holding onto the back of the chair.

"Dat," Miriam insisted and watched over him so he wouldn't fall off.

"Daa," he looked up at her and patted his chubby hands together.

Conveniently, Rosie and Hezekiah pulled into the yard at that moment.

"Mama!" Seth pulled back and forth on the back of the chair in his excitement.

"Dat," Miriam corrected.

"Mama. Daa. Mama. Daa," Seth scrambled off the chair and ran to the door. Minutes later, Rosie came inside. "Mama," Seth was all smiles, then ran to the chair and climbed up to look outside again. "Mama, Daa," he patted his hands together.

Rosie looked at her mother, shocked.

"While you were away, we spent time saying, Daa. It is as close as I could get him to say, Dat."

"*Ach, Mamm*. It's so *gut* to hear him saying something more." Rosie hugged Miriam, tears in her eyes, but Seth's excited "*Mama*, Daa" foretold the men were on their way to the house, and Seth had scrambled off the chair and ran to the door.

When Hezekiah opened the door, Seth was all over him. Picking the little boy up, Hezekiah laughed at the child's energy.

"*Mama*, Daa," Seth grinned broadly and patted Hezekiah's face.

Hezekiah looked from Seth to the women, shocked. "Did he just say, *Dat*?"

Before Rosie or Miriam could answer, Seth giggled. "Daa."

Hezekiah laughed and threw Seth in the air, causing the little boy to squeal his delight at the new game they had begun. "Daa," he hugged Hezekiah around the neck and buried his face into his neck.

Rosie rubbed her son's back, smiling, tears of joy streaming down her cheeks.

Hezekiah wrapped his arm around her and pulled her close. They looked into one another's eyes.
"This is the best Christmas ever," they said together. They laughed at their harmony, knowing their special bond showed they were beginning to think alike.

Miriam smiled at Tobiah, "I'll say! After all, isn't Christmas the season for miracles?

Tobiah leaned closer and kissed Miriam on the cheek. "*Ja. Das* right!"

~ ~ ~

Then was our mouth filled with laughter,
And our tongue with singing'
~ Psalm 126:2 ~

Have you experienced Rosie's History? There is hope!

Domestic abuse is all too common in all societies and cultures and doesn't always leave visible evidence. All forms of abuse are used as a means for one person to maintain power and control over another. There are many types of abuse that can take place in a domestic situation. The more common are: physical, emotional (including isolation and brainwashing), financial, sexual, and verbal.

God loves you and did not create you to be the instrument of another's cruel abuse, nor does He want you to remain in any abusive situation. You are one of His little children. God is love, and love is patient and kind – it does not harm, but uplifts and is joy.

Remember:

Abuse is NEVER your fault, nor is it your responsibility to prevent it. You do not DESERVE to be in <u>ANY</u> unhealthy relationship. Leaving an abuser can be the most empowering and life-saving decision ever.

Fortunately, there is help – **you are not alone!**
If you or someone you know are in an abusive
relationship, simply call:

The National Domestic Abuse Hotline 1-800-799-7233

And someone trained to help others living with domestic
violence will help you. The information offered
through this Hotline is free, confidential, and
could be lifesaving.

You have a responsibility to yourself, and any
children to get out of that abusive situation.

~ ~ ~

It would be better for him that a millstone
Were hanged about his neck,
And he be cast into the sea,
Than he should offend one of My little ones.
~ Like 17:2 ~

Next in the Woodcarver's Quilt series:

HIRAM'S HAPPINESS

Order of Sequence for Reading The
Woodcarver's Quilt Series:

The Woodcarver's Quilt
Esther's Story
A Christmas Rose
Hiram's Happiness